DIRECT APPROACH

BOOK 2

DIRECT APPROACH

CHRISTIAN DRAMAS

BOOK 2

ANNE COLLINS

Kevin Mayhew

First published in 1999 by
KEVIN MAYHEW LTD
Buxhall
Stowmarket
Suffolk
IP14 3BW

© 1999 Anne Collins

The right of Anne Collins to be identified as the author
of this work has been asserted by her in accordance
with the Copyright, Designs and Patents Act 1988.

The scripts within this book may be photocopied by the organisation
which purchases this copy without copyright infringement,
provided they are used for the purpose for which they are intended.
Reproduction of any of the contents of this book for commercial purposes
is subject to the usual copyright restrictions.

No other part of this publication may be reproduced,
stored in a retrieval system, or transmitted, in any form or by any means,
electronic, mechanical, photocopying, recording or otherwise,
without the prior permission of the publisher.

All rights reserved.

0 1 2 3 4 5 6 7 8 9

ISBN 1 84003 442 4
Catalogue No 1500309

Cover illustration by Kirstie Whiteford
Cover design by Jaquetta Sergeant
Edited by Elisabeth Bates

Contents

This book is dedicated to the Glory of God and to
all Mustard Seeds past, present and future.

'Neither he who plants nor he who waters is anything,
but only God, who makes things grow' *1 Corinthians 3:7*

Also by Anne Collins:
Rock Solid – A foundation course in youth drama for worship
Direct Approach, Book One – Christian drama for young people

Acknowledgements

Firstly this book is dedicated to the glory of God. All our gifts come from him and for that we give thanks. This book has been made possible by the dedication of past Mustard Seeds and Mustard Seed International, and by the unending patience of all the members of my family, especially Geoff. Many thanks to Dewi and Alwena for spiritual support during this year and during the time of Mustard Seed, including sleeping in strange places at MAYC conferences! Many thanks to all my friends in Devon and Cornwall.

Introduction

This book combines the approaches to be found in *Rock Solid* and *Direct Approach, Book One*. The sketches are accompanied by Director's tips, for those of you who feel that you need a helping hand in direction. However, the sketches in this book are generally more advanced than those in my previous publications, therefore I decided to include a few games and skills, developing techniques and introduced some new ideas for you to try, some of which are to be found in the introduction to each sketch.

You can just dip in to the games and skills which are appropriate for your group, or for the sketch upon which you are working at any one time. Alternatively, you can just make up your own workshop as a series of fun and skill building activities for any group.

Adults enjoy these activities just as much as young people, so don't restrict your use of this book to young people only. Drama is not only there to be enjoyed by those under eighteen, or just another chance for the youth group to perform, but a valid growing together, fun activity for all ages. If you design your own workshop the length can be determined by the needs of your group, the time available, and the interest of the leader in using games and activities to develop skills. (If you need more ideas then you might like to refer to *Rock Solid – A foundation course in youth drama for worship* and *Direct Approach, Book One – Christian drama for young people (workshops)*, which have many more in-depth ideas, and games.)

Where there is a theme or biblical reference, remember it can be changed and adapted to suit your needs, it is not cast in tablets of stone!

I have found the activities of great benefit during church weekends involving all ages, youth drama workshops, mixed ages preparing sketches for worship and the development of skills for those under ten years old as well. So be brave and experiment!

About the Author

Anne Collins lives in the North of England and has been a teacher for over thirty years. She is married, with two children, both actors. She has retired from teaching as such, but works as an 'Artist in Schools', bringing her experience in drama skills to staff and pupils. From 1985 until 1993 she directed the Mustard Seed Drama Fellowship (an ecumenical group including young people from all denominations, plus those searching for faith), which appeared twice at MAYC, in the Westminster Central Hall, firstly with sketches similar to those in this book, and secondly with a production of *The Man*, a multimedia rock musical paralleling conditions of the world, with the person of Jesus Christ, and challenging all to 'stand up and be counted' alongside him against injustice, prejudice and cruelty. She was also involved in Youth Theatre Workshops, writing full-scale productions with a message, such as *Travelling Light*, *Snow Queen* (With God all things are possible), *Pinocchio* (New life is available for all), *Alice* (Be as a little child), creating original nativity scripts for church and school, and, as Head of Drama in a variety of schools, teaching. Her ministry with Mustard Seed included leading services, church weekends, and Drama in Worship courses. From this has arisen her latest project, 'Sowing Seeds', a kind of 'have workshop, will travel' idea. She also runs, along with Geoff, her husband, 'Drama Workshop', for young people aged eight upwards, which homes-in on drama skills, builds confidence and creates a good group experience for those involved. She and her husband attend St Andrew's Methodist Church in Bolton.

She hopes that this book, written from her experience, will be of use to those who feel called to communicate God's word through drama, and especially to support those who are afraid to make the first move because of lack of confidence.

Develop Your Skills

Some useful drama activities

Warm-up

Shakeout – Cassette and/or CD player required

- Using a popular CD or cassette with a good medium-to-fast rhythm, all stand in a space and shake out hands, arms, legs, hips, face.
- Shake right hand, then left hand, feet, hips, shoulders, head and whole body in time to the music. Stretch high, touch toes (Mr Motivator's got nothing on this!) at least ten times.
- Roll head round slowly to the left in a full circle, then to the right. Repeat five times each.
- Slowly, vertebra by vertebra (beginning with the base of the neck and working down), bend from the waist. Then swing arms to the right and to the left five times each, finally slowly uncurl to standing position, vertebra by vertebra, beginning at the base of the spine.
- Move into a circle, and each member of the group devises a simple (but energetic, please) movement which is copied by the others. You can add to this by making it mobile. Move around the room, copying the leader, who keeps changing the moves.
- Stress energy here, much leaping and jumping is required to loosen up.

Stick in the Mud: a warm-up game

All in a space. One or two people are 'on'. The others must dodge around the room without being 'tigged'. If they are caught, they must stand with feet apart and arms outstretched. They can be released by someone crawling under their legs.

Any game which requires running and exertion can be used to precede or follow the shakeout, as long as they are encouraged to use different parts of the body, and to bend and stretch and not remain on one level, twitching gently! It must be full of ENERGY!

Breathing and relaxation (10-15 min)

Play a quiet piece of music during this exercise

- All to lie flat on backs in a space away from each other. It is important that they are relaxed with eyes closed, hands by sides, fingers unclenched, legs uncrossed and feet flopping outwards. Take a deep breath, and imagine your ribs expanding as the air streams down your throat and fills your lungs, entering your blood and refreshing the old, used air.
- The leader asks them to think about their bodies, how they are made up, and how they function. Think of the veins and arteries pumping blood around the body; lungs exchanging fresh air for polluted air; stomach digesting food; the energy in the brain sending signals like an electric current; your ears as a mini audio system accepting sound; the nervous system sensing the hardness of the floor and linking together all the sensations of the body.

It is important that the leader's voice is soft and calming and not intrusive as the instructions are given. There might be some giggles, especially at the mention of the digestive system! But remind them of the 'One body'. You could quietly read the passage from 1 Corinthians 12:12-26 as they concentrate.

- Ask them to focus solely on one bodily activity while lying completely relaxed. For example, feel the blood pumping round the body. These are *actual* sensations that are really happening. Give them two or three minutes to really focus on this. You might suggest a few for them to choose from, for example, perspiration, pulse, digestion, heartbeat (blood sucked into one chamber, pushed into the next, and then squeezed into the vein or artery), breathing, indigestion.
- Still speaking quietly, get them to think of things that they can't actually sense happening, but which they know are occurring all the time almost secretly. Then imagine them

happening. Give them these examples: hair growing, nails growing, spots bursting through the skin, germs fighting antibodies in the bloodstream, skin flaking and peeling, germs attacking the teeth, air in the blood, kidneys filtering the poisons from the body.

- Finally ask them to breathe in as deeply as they can, and slowly exhale. Do this five or six times.

Stretch, relax

It is important that they are aware of the different feelings between tension and relaxation. It is good to make them think about it, and notice the different sensations at this time.

- Still lying down, ask them to stretch their hands taut, and then relax them. Work through the body isolating as far as possible each set of muscles, stretching and relaxing them. Hands, hands and arms, feet, feet and legs, stomach muscles, shoulders, chest, neck, and finally all face muscles (open eyes and mouth wide, stretch tongue, etc.).
- Finally stretch the whole body and relax, twice. *Slowly* sit up. Stand in **neutral**.

Voice

Chewy Toffee Tongue Twisters

- Explain that the mouth is like a cavern which echoes with any sound, and that it is important to use it as a sounding board. Remind them that often we must speak in places where it is difficult to be heard and we must make maximum use of our voices. These exercises help us to speak more clearly and to project our voices better. Do this as they work through the exercise.
- In a circle, leader joining in, imagine that you have a very large piece of toffee in your mouth. Chew it, stretching jaws, etc. This will cause great amusement at first, but encourage self-control! Stick tongue out as far as possible (much dribbling here – be prepared), touch chin, nose, then right cheek, followed by left cheek. Repeat several times. Say the following with tongue stretched out:

Plain bun, plum bun,
bun without a plum,
plain bun, plum bun,
bun without a plum.

- Still with tongue out, say it
  a. as if it is a great joke
  b. angrily
  c. slowly to a foreigner!
- Repeat again (with tongue *in* this time), emphasising the mood *without* losing the beginnings and ends of words. Clear diction required. Speed it up as fast as you can to finish.
- Emphasise the need for clear speech and good diction, and full use of the muscles in the face and tongue. You can use any rhymes you know for this exercise.

Concentration and focus – a soft ball needed

Focus Freeze (10-15 min)

- Explain that this game is to improve concentration skills and to get the group to focus on their physical energy and the control of it, and to distinguish between points of high energy and points where the energy level flags. As the ball is thrown and caught, there is one instant when all our energy is focused. This is called the high point of energy.
- In a circle, throw a soft ball to one another, make sure everyone has a throw and a catch. Keep it going until there is a rhythm. Call out the name of the person to whom you are throwing, and gain eye contact.
- Try to find each person's high point of energy as they throw and catch the ball. In order to do this, ask each person to 'freeze' at the point of high energy for two seconds after they have thrown the ball, and the catcher freezes for two seconds after or as he/she catches the ball.

The tendency is that people will hold the point of energy for a split second and then relax slightly to freeze. Stop them and point this out. As they continue, the throws and catches should become full of energy and the physicality of the group will be improved. If the ball is dropped, still freeze on the highest point of energy. Draw the parallel with putting on a sketch or play –

too often we play a sketch below the full level of energy, and it loses focus. It therefore does not have the impact it should have on the audience. A bit like life really! We often perform in many areas just below our full capability, because of lack of confidence, carelessness, laziness or perhaps to save ourselves stress! I often catch myself doing this! Do you? Well, here's your opportunity to be focused!

Quick pics and introducing levels

Quick pics

- Divide the group into threes or fours.
- Give them 15 seconds to create a visual image of the themes listed below. (Leader counts down the seconds). On the count of 15 the command **freeze** is given, and the leader gives points to the best three. A tambour drum comes in handy here as a signal. (It saves your voice!)

  Themes:
  All groups: teapot, accident, party, car, boat.
  Individual groups: (Given a card with their quick pic on it. Keep it secret) Noah building the boat, tower, temple, house, cathedral.

Levels

- The use of levels is quite a simple concept. It means using different physical positions at different heights. For example, lying flat on the floor is the lowest level, stretching up, standing on tiptoe is the highest level, standing normally is the middle level, and the other levels are points in between.
- These can be achieved purely by the actors' physical position in relation to each other, or can be enhanced with the use of chairs, blocks, pews, pulpit, or whatever is at hand. As we look at a picture, our eye is drawn around it by the placing of various objects, and/or their colour.
- We focus on a contrast, or something towards which the objects or people are gesturing or pointing. In order to do this, and to lead the eye of the beholder towards that which we want them to view (*that* was a mouthful!), we place people and things at different levels.

Sharing (10-15 min)

- Let each group show their individual **Quick Pic**, and get the rest to guess the theme, then talk about the merits of each group.
- Importance of physical contact without embarrassment.
- Working efficiently, no time to argue.
- Using imagination, in the use of **levels.**
- Being open to the ideas of others.
- **Freeze** means *no* movement at all.
- Introduction of the term **visual image,** with reference to adverts and symbols of modern life.

Develop some style: melodrama

Equipment needed: box containing various hats, props and clothes for characterisation.

Characterisation

(For further work on characterisation see *Rock Solid – A foundation course in youth drama for worship*)

- At this point, talk to them about characters. Explain what characterisation is (see *Glossary*), and how we can stereotype people. Melodrama has stereotypical characters and usually a set format (see *Glossary*).

  Villain: One of the Upper Classes. Wears cloak and top hat, has moustache (for twirling), stalks the stage with an exaggerated step, the epitome of evil!

  Heroine: Sweet and simpering, given to sudden fainting and exclamations of 'Woe is me'. Exaggerated movement, many sighs. Has an aura of innocence.

  Father: Wears a cap, doffed frequently to the Villain. Usually in an alcoholic haze, with a violent temper when under the influence, and likely to beat his daughter.
- Experiment with two or three characters from melodrama. Ask them all to make a statue of the villain, twirl moustache, swirl imaginary cloak.
- On a given signal (a drum beat is effective), the group move around the space 'in character', changing direction on command.
- Try the Heroine in the same way, statue, then horrified expressions, using exaggerated body

language and facial expression. Walking daintily. (The boys will have a ball with this one!)

- Do a similar exercise with the Father. (It might be useful here to input a little about Victorian values, and the problems of the working classes. A discussion about the uses and abuses of alcohol might emerge from this at a later date?)
- Tip: It is useful to keep a box of hats, wigs, items of clothing props such as handbags, umbrellas, fans, etc., as it can often be used to inspire a character, or become a focus for an idea. Sometimes it can become an integral part of the sketch. Please note that I am not talking about full costume here, just suggestions – a hat, a pair of gloves, a mask, an umbrella, etc.
- Give one or two items to each member of the group and ask them to sit in a space with one item of costume or object connected with Melodrama placed on either side of them. You will need more items than there are members of the group, to give some flexibility.
- Ask them to stand and on a given signal (a drum beat is effective), the group move around the space, changing direction on command.
- On hearing a double drum beat they stop and pick up a prop or piece of clothing, sit down, and think about a character the object or clothing suggests. Tell them to close their eyes and begin to create their character around the object. Think about age, looks, attitude, clothing, voice, way of walking, etc., put the card face down on the floor. When they are ready, and in their own time, they make a frozen statue of the character.
- Then ask them to *move* as the character, paying attention to the personality and age, occupation and attitude of the character they have created.
- Freeze them on a drumbeat and ask them to imagine that their character has a sound, *not* words, just a sound, it may be high, low, smooth, aggressive, frightened, cheeky, bossy, etc. Choose a sound that could best represent their character. Remind them of voice, posture, attitude and so on.
- Then again, on the signal, they move **in character** (meaning no distraction or watching others – total concentration) and add the *sound* of their personality. Stop them again and ask them to imagine their character in a normal situation, as the Victorians and Edwardians, in melodrama, stereotyped the 'working classes' and the 'upper classes'. Emphasise keeping 'in character' all the time, and not being distracted by others. If everyone concentrates on their own work then no one is being watched. This is all a part of building each other up. (Ephesians 4:16)
- Everything is often seen in black and white without the shades of grey which exist! So in this instance they are after stereotypes, as the Victorians and Edwardians, in melodrama, portrayed stereotypical 'working classes' and the 'upper classes'.
- Then ask them to imagine what their character might be thinking or saying in that situation. On the next signal they move and speak the thought track or speech track of that character. All do this together, as it avoids embarrassment for the shy members of the group.
- Finally **freeze** them again and ask them to turn to the nearest person and have a conversation with them, again, keeping **in character.**
- If the group is confident enough you can explain that you are going to freeze them again and ask them to continue their conversation when you tap one of them on the shoulder. Let each couple have a go, but if anyone is too nervous, or hasn't much to say, just freeze them again and go on to the next pair.
- If someone is deliberately fooling about which sometimes happens, tell them in no uncertain terms that they are being destructive, but try to assess why they are behaving this way before you wade in too heavily, for giggles and laughter often are signs of embarrassment and nerves.

Noah's Rainbow

An introduction

CHARACTERS

Chorus A/Dove	*Chorus B*	*Chorus C/Noah*	*Chorus D*
Chorus E/Irritating child	*Chorus F/Raven*	*Reader*	

THEME Genesis 6, 7, 8:1-19

Covering the story of Noah from the point when the boat is completed and the flood begins, up to the appearance of the rainbow. This sketch goes down very well with audiences of any age, but is particularly useful in family services.

APPROACH

- This sketch is in the style of song and dance and relies for its humour on slick, well-timed movement. All the chorus need to be able to change character easily, and each character or object must be definite and distinguishable from the others. (See *Characterisation* in *Develop Your Skills*.)
- Some work on body language and characterisation would be useful prior to rehearsal. (See *Rock Solid – A foundation course in youth drama for worship* for further ideas.) The whole sketch must be overexaggerated, and should draw the audience into the tongue-in-cheek approach. The pace of the piece should be quite fast, with characters jumping in on cues.
- Clarity of diction vital, especially in the musical sections. (See *Chewy Toffee Tongue Twisters* in *Develop Your Skills*.)
- Rubber faces needed!

A face exercise for fun

Grinny

- It is useful to explain here, that face muscles are vital not only in the production of the voice, but also in the control of changing facial expressions. People always work better when they know the reasons for their work, don't you think?
- Ask them to grin and then make their mouths into a large 'yawn-shaped' hole. Then immediately grin again, followed by a 'whistling-shaped' hole. Repeat this several times.
- It helps if the leader says the words 'Grin, small hole. Grin, large hole', as they do this, to keep the speed up.
- Follow up with Chewy Toffee Tongue Twisters using another rhyme such as 'Peter Piper picked a peck of pickled pepper', or 'Red lorry, yellow lorry'. All very good for improving articulation!

Stage falls

As there are often 'falls' within the sketches, it is useful here to teach the basics of falling without damage! First, the simplest way which is the best for beginners:

- Fall onto knees, then onto the side of the thighs and buttocks, and let the rest of the body relax and fall and unfold naturally, head last. Totally relax.

  Practise a couple of times, slowly at first, then speed up the action.

Noah's Rainbow

Genesis 6, 7, 8:1-19

	(All are in a straight line upstage with backs to the audience. The Reader is DSL) (**1**)
Reader	*(DSR)* God looked down on the earth, and saw that there was much evil. When he saw how wicked people were he was sorry that he had ever made mankind. He was so filled with regret that he said, 'I will wipe out all these people I have created. But the Lord was pleased with Noah. He told Noah to build a boat, and to take his wife and his three sons and two of every animal and bird into the boat. Noah did everything he had been commanded. *(Reader exits)*
Chorus D	*(Turning to audience)* And suddenly . . . (**2**)
All	(Turn and gasp, freezing in horrified positions) (**3**)
Chorus D	The sky became overcast . . .
All	*(Look up)* (**4**)
Chorus D	. . . and turned a sort of deathly dark colour. (**5**)
Chorus F	The clouds ripped.
All	*(Ripping sound and action)*
Chorus F	In two . . . and the wrath of God rang out.
All	Ding! (**6**)
Chorus C	There was a loud CRACK.
All	CRACK! (**7**)
Chorus C	And the heavens opened.
All	Creeeeak! (**8**)

Director's Tips

(**1**) Freeze in position at the beginning. All should be standing in NEUTRAL (see *Glossary*). Never begin until you are sure that you have the attention of the audience.

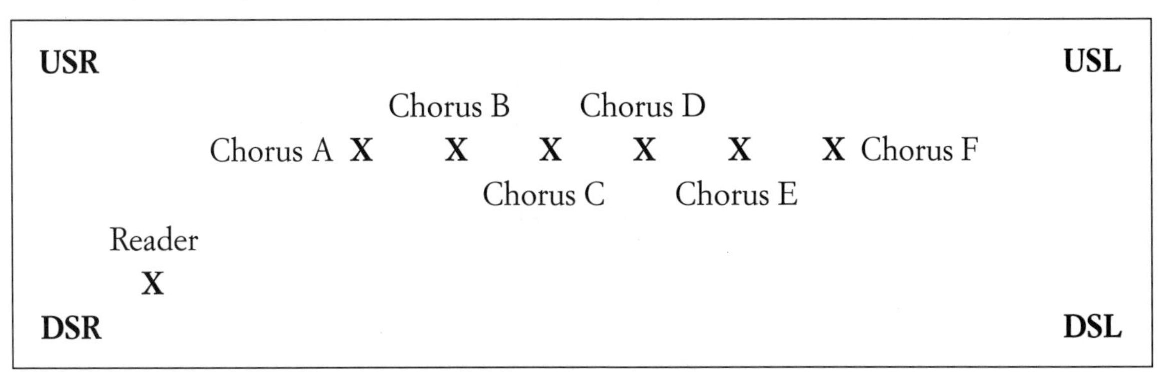

(**2**) Turn with a big and positive movement. Make it highly dramatic to hold the attention of the audience. Emphasise the reaction of the rest of the group, setting the tone for the whole sketch.

(**3**) Devise a QUICK PIC for this horrified group. (See *Develop Your Skills.*) Remember LEVELS give it visual impact. The body language must show shock magnified, not half-hearted horror!

(**4**) Look up in horror at exactly the same time. Use 'overcast' as your cue which will keep the pace going, rather than waiting until the word is spoken.

(**5**) Stand fearfully in line, as at the beginning, on the words 'and the sky turned', and ready for movement! By 'ripped' all should have turned to SR. On 'ripped' imagine you have a piece of cloth in front of you. Hold it, both hands together, and on 'ripped', wildly tear it, so that hands are stretched wide, at the same time, in unison, turn faces to audience with wide-eyed look of horror.

(**6**) Bring right foot next to left foot with feet slightly apart. Raise right hand and pull imaginary bell rope. All this must be done on the word 'Ding!' Make sure that everyone has a wide and very silly grin on their face. Hopefully, by this time, the audience will raise a titter! We hope!

(**7**) Clap on the second crack. Facial expression one of horror.

(**8**) On 'creeeeak' all move hands slowly apart and move right foot back so that you go back to the previous SR position. See (**5**).

Chorus A	*(Moving to kneel in front of group)* The thunder roared ferociously. (**9**)
All	*(Roar weakly)* (**10**)
Chorus A	*(Critically shouting)* Ferociously . . .
All	*(Roar ferociously)* (**11**)
Chorus C	And the lightning singed the earth.
All	*(Pointing at Chorus A)* Sssssssinge! (**12**)
Chorus E	*(Action)* The rain poured down in torrents. (**13**)
Chorus B	And umbrellas popped up everywhere. (**14**)
Chorus D	Pop!
Chorus F	Pop! (**15**)
Chorus E	Pop!
Chorus C	Pop!
Chorus B	Pop!
Chorus A	Pop!
Chorus D	It was the biggest. *(Turn to audience)* (**16**)
Chorus F	Most terriblest. *(Turn to audience)*
Chorus C	Scariest. *(Turn to audience)*
Chorus A	Worstest. *(Turn to audience)*
Chorus B	LOUDEST! *(Turn to audience)*
Chorus E	Drenchingest. *(Turn to audience)*
All	*(Action)* **Storm** the **world** had **ever**, **ever**, **ever seen**. *(To audience)* (**17**)

(9) Run to position kneeling in front of the group with hands over ears. The pace must not be slowed by slow positioning. So as soon as the creak move is finished Chorus A moves. The others can hold the position a second longer.

(10) All turn and roar half-heartedly. Chorus A looks at them critically and shouts 'Ferociously'.

(11) As if suddenly galvanised into action all roar with wildly exaggerated ferocity, echoed in voice and body. Make it look interesting too – remember LEVELS? (See *Quick Pics* in *Develop Your Skills.*)

(12) A sudden attacking movement towards A who reacts as if having a violent electric shock. This can be used as an excuse to move back to original position for the next line. Don't make this last too long, 2-3 seconds of shock is quite enough!

(13) In line again, all facing the audience. Hands up on 'rain', slowly bring them to waist level with wiggly finger 'it's raining' type movements. (See any infant class representing rain and you'll be about right!)

(14) Chorus B cheerfully mimes putting up an umbrella and testing for rain on the word 'popped'. Hold position until all the others have 'Popped'!

(15) All put up umbrella as (**14**). Try to overlap the 'pops' to keep the pace up, and each think of a different reaction to rain. Show this through facial expression, body language, and make the group interesting to look at. This is difficult because you are all in line, so step out of it slightly to form a QUICK PIC of umbrella time!

(16) Use this as an opportunity to get back into line. Speak the words as if telling the story to a little child in over-exaggerated way. Get eye contact with the audience as if willing them to go along with you in this foolish story telling!

(17) There are six words emphasised in this line. Use each one to move both arms into a position stretching above your heads. Position 1: elbows bent at waist, palms upwards; 2: parallel with shoulders; 3: parallel with ears; 4: parallel with top of head, etc., until hands are stretched way above heads. Time it so that each move is in unison.

All *(Sung to 'Singing in the rain')*
Dooby do **doo** dooby **doo**by **doop** doooby dooby
dooby do **doo** dooby **doo**by do **doo**.
We're singing in the **rain,**
we'll **never** be the same,
what a **fright**ening feeling! It's . . .
really a pain.

I don't think it will stop,
it **goes plipp**etty **plopp**etty **plipp**etty **PLOP,**
we're **drown**ing, just drowning **in the**
dooby do **doo** dooby **doo**by **doop** doooby dooby
dooby do **doo** dooby **doo**by do **doo**.

Old **Noah**'s got a **boat,**
it **really** gets my **goat,**
what a **frust**rating feeling
that **he'll** stay afloat.
If **only we'**d been **good,**
God **would**n't **have sent this flood,**
we're drowning, just drowning in the **rain.** (**18**)

Chorus D *(Spoken)* And suddenly . . .

Chorus A, C, F *(Become trees)* (**19**)

Chorus D *(Looking at the trees)* All the tropical rain forests.

Chorus E *(Becomes Mount Everest)* And Mount Everest. (**20**)

Chorus B *(Becomes Empire State Building)* And even the Empire State Building. (**21**)

Chorus D *(Melodramatically)* Disappeared.

All Glug glug glug glug glug glug glug glug! (**22**)

Chorus D *(Makes half a window with both arms)* (**23**)

Chorus C And all that could be seen.

Chorus B *(Makes half a window with both arms, trapping C's head)* Was Noah's Ark. (**24**)

(**18**) See *Appendix* for suggested moves for this song.

(**19**) Using the cue 'Suddenly', make grotesque tree shapes and freeze in position. Remember LEVELS? (See *Develop Your Skills.*)

(**20**) Could just stand on tiptoe and make mountain shape with arms and hands, or can jump onto a chair to give extra height and look extremely pleased with him/her self.

(**21**) Stretch high with arms up, pressed against ears, and freeze, looking very uncomfortable.

(**22**) All bend knees to squatting position, as if the waters are rising to cover them. Rubber faces here with exaggerated 'drowning' expressions.

(**23**)(**24**)To make the window Chorus B and D turn to face each other, join upstage hands above Chorus C's head, then join downstage hands below C's chin, so that C cannot remove head. It can be effective if the window is made at the same time, with Noah voluntarily sticking his/her head out. The window can then reduce in size. Experiment with what works best for you.

Chorus C	*(To audience, cheerfully)* With Noah's head sticking out of the window.
Chorus E	As he viewed the weather. *(Grinning, sits cross-legged in front of 'window' DSC)*
Chorus C	View! *(Look right)* View! *(Look left)* (**25**)
Chorus B	*(Ominously)* Forty days and forty nights, Noah's head.
Chorus C	*(Angry and petulant)* Stayed . . . stuck in the window. (**26**)
Chorus B	*(Dramatically)* And suddenly. (**27**)
All	*(Sung to 'Raining in my heart', Buddy Holly)* (**28**) The sun came out, the sky turned blue, there's not a cloud to spoil the view, it's stopped raining.
Chorus E	*(Stands and dances as he sings 'Singing in the Rain')* (**29**) **Doo**by do **doo** dooby **doo**by **doop** doooby dooby *(Loudly)* **Doo**by do **doo** dooby **doo**by do **doo**.
Chorus B, C, D	*(Kicking E who falls and sulks again)* It's *stopped* raining . . .
All	*(Spoken rhythmically)* Two little birdies sat upon the ark, (**30**) one was a raven, one was a dove.
Chorus E	*(Jumping up accusingly) That* doesn't rhyme.
All	*(Annoyed) So?* (**31**)
Chorus D	*(Sitting down sulkily) So . . .*
All	*(Except E who sulks. Spoken rhythmically)* Fly away raven, find a bit o' land (**32**) come back here with a twig in your hand, stroke beak! *(Look puzzled) (Chorus A, as Raven, exits across SL)* (**33**) *One* little birdie sat upon the ark . . .
Chorus B	*(Shaking head in exaggerated sadness)* The raven hadn't come back!

(25) Exaggerated turning of the head by C, with painful expression. Rubber face again!

(26) Chorus C folds arms and assumes violently angry/sulky expression.

(27) All turn to face the audience on 'Suddenly' (except E who does not join in as he/she becomes grumpy and sulking. This is important as it underlines a later event in which he tries to get the better of everyone.)

(28) The sun came out
Right hand describes a balletic circle and finishes arm stretched, palm upwards.

The sky turned blue
Left hand describes balletic circle finishing arm stretched, palm upwards. Both hands in the air.

There's not a cloud
Right hand to forehead, as if looking in distance, whole body leaning to right.

To spoil the view
Left hand to forehead, as if looking in distance, whole body leaning to left.

It's stopped raining
Hands by sides looking at audience and shrugging shoulders, exactly in unison.

(29) Chorus E deliberately interrupts, showing off and very loud, the others react with exasperated looks. E can improvise his/her own very exaggerated movements here. Very much 'over the top'.

(30) After the violence of the kick (which must look real but not be real!) a smug, polite smile to the audience as if pretending that nothing has happened, sets the mood for the following corny rhyme. All bend elbows and flap hands on level with ears to symbolise birds. This must be done very seriously and look very silly! On 'One was a raven' turn fingers towards ears and make open and shut beak shape in rhythm with words. Then repeat with left hand on 'One was a dove'. This is definitely to be seen as a 'rip take' of children's story time programmes hosted by patronising presenters!

(31) All leaning towards E aggressively. His reaction is to sit down again sulkily defeated, perhaps with arms folded and exaggerated bottom lip problem, like a little child who can't have what he/she wants!

(32) As (**30**).

(33) Chorus A 'flies' across in front of the others, using slow wing movements, and exits SL. All the time she/he looks at the audience like a child showing off onstage. The others follow her across with an exaggerated head movement and a lean towards SL. Then, all facing the audience once more, to continue the rhyme.

Chorus C, D *(Together)* So they still didn't know whether there was any land there. (**34**)

Chorus E *(Smugly)* That *definitely* doesn't rhyme!

Chorus B, C, D *(Leaning aggressively towards E)* So?

Chorus F *(Cheerfully ignoring E)* Sooooo . . . (**35**)

Chorus B, C, D Fly away dove, find a bit o' land (**36**)
come back here with a twig in your hand, stroke wing, stroke beak!

(Dove speedily returns and hands twig to Chorus C) (**37**)

Chorus B, D *(To audience)* Oooooh! *That* was quick!

Chorus E *(Standing and looking up and out to audience)* LOOOOK! (**38**)

All *(Move back to starting positions)*
Up above the ark and animals (**39**)
way up in the sky,
there was placed a beautiful rainbow
that came from God on high.
R – A – I – N – B – O – W.
The rainbow is a symbol showing
God's promise to you.
He will always keep you safe
if you're faithful, good and true.
R – A – I – N – B – O – W.

(FREEZE) (**40**)

(34) Exaggerated sadness, shaking head exactly as Chorus B in the previous speech.

(35) As F speaks he/she changes into 'dove' with gentle flapping of 'wings'.

(36) All turn towards F, indicating her with left hand, all at the same time of course! A quizzical expression might help here. Dove 'flies' across SR in front of them, and keeping the left hand extended they swivel to the right as if following. Remain frozen with hand outstretched until dove returns, which is immediate. E, still sitting, begins to show a little interest.

(37) Dove flies to Chorus C, hands over twig, and then resumes original position and chorus character. E turns to look at twig, still on low level.

(38) All gather round and look at the same spot as E. If desired, A can rush on here to join them. Great excitement in their facial expressions. Hold the amazed tableau (Remember LEVELS!) for no longer than 2 seconds, then immediately back to original positions as at the start, for song.

(39) (Sung to *Rainbow* from the children's TV programme of that name)

Up above the ark and animals (**39**)
Point finger of right hand, with arm by side, slowly raise it to indicate rainbow.

Way up in the sky
Hand should be raised and pointing, arm stretched to full by 'sky'.

There was placed a beautiful rainbow
Turn hand palm upwards. Bring arm down to just below shoulder level, to audience.

That came from God on high
Arm slowly down to side by 'God'. Heads look up on 'high'.

R – A – I – N – B – O – W
(A) (B) (C) (D) (E) (F) (All)
All step forward on right foot, one at a time, hand outstretched to audience, Vaudeville style, on a letter of the word. Remain in position until 'W'. On 'W' all stand straight and raise both hands to form the shape of the letter. Hands and arms stretched.

The rainbow is a symbol showing
Bring hands slowly down, palms up.

God's promise to you
Cross right hand over chest on 'prom' and left over right on 'you'.

He will always keep you safe
Lean confidentially towards audience, arms still across chest in the style of the best dancing school tradition!

If you're faithful, good and true.
With right hand pointing, wag finger three times on 'faith' to right, on 'good' to centre and on 'true' to left.

R – A – I – N – B – O – W. As before

(40) Hold freeze for at least three seconds at the end and allow the audience to begin applause.

(33) [illegible]

(34) [illegible]

(35) [illegible]

(36) [illegible]

(38) All [illegible] and look at the [illegible]

(39) Song of Rainbow from the children's TV program [illegible]

Up above the ark and animals (39)
[illegible]

High in the sky
[illegible]

[illegible]

The sign from God so [illegible]
[illegible]

[illegible]

[illegible]

[illegible]

[illegible]

(40) [illegible]

Jo Narr
An introduction

CHARACTERS

Narrator 1   *Narrator 2*   *Jo Narr*   *Chorus 1*   *Chorus 2*   *Chorus 3*

THEME Jonah 1, 2, 3:2-5

The story of Jonah and the whale set in modern times, from the time when Jonah runs away from God, to the miracle of Nineveh.

APPROACH

- This is a sketch dependent upon physicality, body language and facial expression. It should move quickly, with actors jumping in on cues.
- It's a fun sketch, with a lot to say about our attitude to prayer, and the way we ignore that still, small voice when it is booming in our ears!
- It is well worth spending a fair amount of time on the moves, to synchronise them and to make them slick.

Develop some style: storyboarding

- Read the story of Jonah together. Discuss the story and its meaning then when it was written, and its meaning for us now. Pose the question, 'What is your Nineveh?' and share your feelings.
- Sometimes this approach to exploring the Bible and one's own relationship with God can be a real release for burdens, and questions. It is well worth anticipating some of the things which might come up. (It's useful to have paper and pens handy.)
- First they must split the story into sections and list the key points. For example: 1. God speaks to Jonah and he doesn't want to hear; 2. Jonah tries to escape from God by sailing away. This is called **Storyboarding** and is a useful way to approach all improvisations of stories from the Bible.
- In groups of three to five use the main points and make a tableau for each to illustrate the story. The scene can be set in biblical times, or in modern times. Give them 15 to 20 minutes to complete. Make sure that all the pictures are covered! Be available to help groups when necessary . . . so check up on your theology here, or call in an expert to help. A good commentary on Jonah would be a useful accessory!
- Watch each other's 'Storyboards' and discuss good points, and ways they might be improved. Congratulate accurate mime, use of levels and good freeze techniques, etc.
- Discuss ways of improvement. Always encourage the group to be positive and constructive in their criticisms, so go for the good things first. Encourage truthful but generous comment at all times, then look at the negative things under the umbrella of possible improvements. This is a much less threatening way of dealing with presentations. 'It's not what you say . . . it's the way that you say it!'

Some things to think about

- Is the visual communication accurate? Is it telling the story?
- Is the mime believable? Are the group really concentrating?
- Are they making the best use of levels?
- Is there evidence of good group co-operation?

Jo Narr

(Narrators are DSR and DSL of family group who are frozen in a family portrait of Jo, wife and children) (**1**)

Narrator 1 Jo Narr . . .

Jo Narr *(Jo and Chorus 1 come to life)* Hey! *(Returning to freeze)* (**2**)

Narrator 1 Was a bank clerk . . . who lived in *Bolton* town. His life was uneventful . . . (**3**)

Jo Narr *(Shrug shoulders changing position)* And it never gets me down!

Chorus 1 *(As 'wife' clinging to Jo Narr's arm)* His wife was tall and frumpy! (**4**)

Chorus 2, 3 *(As caricature 'kids' clinging to Jo and Wife)* His kids were small and dumpy. (**5**)

Narrator 2 Jo Narr . . .

Jo Narr *(Smug)* Hey! (**6**)

Narrator 2 Was . . .

Jo Narr *(Interrupting and moving DSCR)* Very, very happy with life the way it was!

(Chorus 1, 2 and 3 form shape of car) (**7**)

Narrator 1 Upon one Sunday morning, as Jo Narr cleaned his car. *(Jo cleans car)* (**8**)

Narrator 2 A voice from heaven called him . . . said . . .

All Chorus *(All Chorus become 'God' and make 'stop' gesture to Jo Narr as they speak)* STOP right where you are! (**9**)

Jo Narr *(Looks worried)* (**10**)

Director's Tips

Starting positions

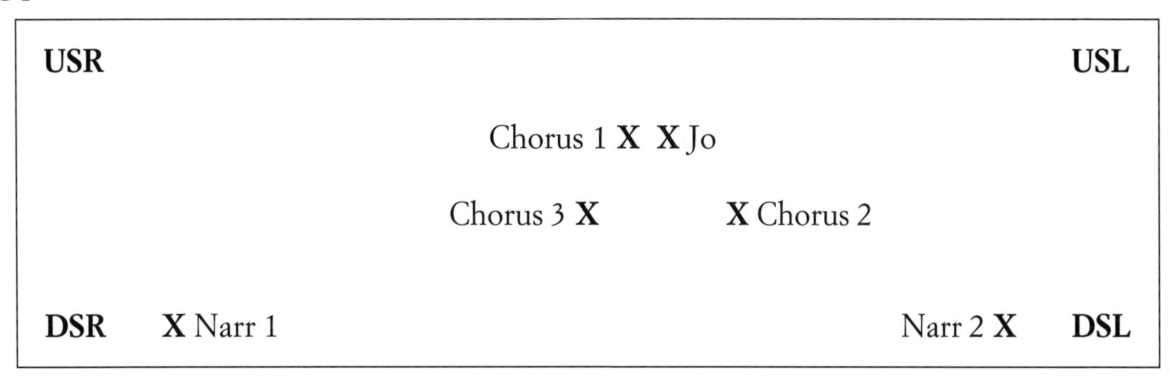

(**1**) The family portrait should be rather smug with a slightly henpecked Jo Narr, a wife hanging on to his arm in a clinging manner, and two children, clutching at their parents on either side.

(**2**) Leaning forward out of the tableau with a thumbs-up sign, and a confidently cheerful tone of voice. Then immediately back to 'freeze'. The family should not move at all.

(**3**) Steps forward from the group slightly as he speaks, shrugging his shoulders.

(**4**) Interrupting Narrator as 'wife' with appropriate voice, clinging again to Jo's arm possessively.

(**5**) As Narrator speaks the other Chorus 2 and 3, still as caricature children, move to Jo and Chorus 1, clutching them as before. It is vital that they stay frozen until this point so that they do not draw focus away from the main action. All freeze as before.

(**6**) See (**2**).

(**7**) On the cue 'was', Chorus 1, 2 and 3 form shape of car CS. How do we make the shape of a car, you ask? (See *Quick Pics* in *Develop Your Skills*)

(**8**) Jo *energetically* mimes cleaning car. (For more help with this see Mime sections and Essence Machines in *Rock Solid – A foundation course in youth drama for worship*)

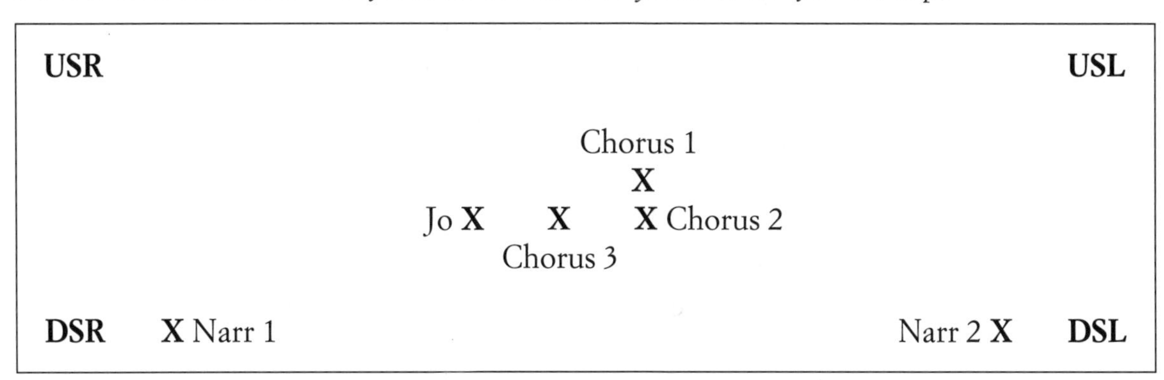

(**9**) Chorus 1, 2 and 3 kneel up and gesture commandingly as they speak, with downstage hand, arm outstretched and palm towards Jo who should retreat SR in shock.

(**10**) Change of facial expression from shock to worry.

Chorus 1	*(As God)* You really must not worry.
Chorus 2	*(As God)* To Blackpool you must hurry.
Chorus 3	For **in** that **place**.
All Chorus	*(Rhythmically)* I'm **most** un**ha**ppy with **things** the **way** they **are**! (**11**)
Narrator 1	Jo Narr . . .
Jo Narr	Hey? *(Looks very puzzled)* (**12**)
Narrator 1	Was very puzzled.
Jo Narr	What for? (**13**)
Narrator 2	He said . . .
Jo Narr	*(Sulkily)* Why me?
Chorus 1	*(Stand)* They must stop playing Bingo. (**14**)
Chorus 2	*(Kneel)* And pray on bended knee. (**14**)
Chorus 3	*(Stand and wag finger)* They're full of sin . . . and greedy. (**14**)
All Chorus	With no care for the needy. (**14**)
Narrator 2	But Jo Narr . . .
Jo Narr	Hey! *(Irritated)* (**15**)
Narrator 2	Was very, very happy with life the way it was.
Jo Narr	*(Moves SR sulky and stubborn)* I will not go! *(Like a petulant child)*
Narrator 1	Said Jo Narr.
All Chorus	*(All standing)* Oh yes you will! (**16**)
Narrator 1	God said.

(11) This is most effective when spoken in a sing-song rhythm, with the emphasis on the words in bold type, almost as if the Chorus is making fun of Jonah! A hand movement to left and right on the rhythm helps. The Narrators can join in too!

(12) 'Hey' is Jo Narr's catchword. However, each time he says it differently. The audience, by this time, is anticipating it and you should expect a titter of amusement each time it crops up. This time it is with extreme bewilderment. Note that on a question the voice rises slightly at the end of a sentence.

(13) The next two speeches should be spoken like a teenager, angry with parents for making them do something they don't want to do.

(14) This must be articulated clearly. (See *Chewy Toffee Tongue Twisters* in *Develop Your Skills,* which can be adapted by using words in the script.) Chorus, as the voice of God, must be commanding.

(15) 'Hey', irritated, and then little boy sulky as he moves away.

(16) Wagging fingers at him.

Jo Narr *(Turning to them)* Oh no I won't. (**17**)

All Chorus Oh yes you will!

Jo Narr *(Turning away sulkily)* Oh no I won't. *(All continue ad lib until interrupted)*

Narrator 1 *(Moving towards them, waving arms)* All right. All right. Cut the theatricals! *(Pause for reaction. Then moves to Narr 2 DSL)* God would not leave poor Jo alone . . . and Jo . . . (**18**)

Jo Narr *(Clutching his stomach and grimacing in pain)* Hey! (**19**)

Narrator 2 Became quite ill. *(Jo moves CS, kneels, mimes packing his holdall)* (**20**)

Narrator 1 He quickly packed his holdall. *(Jo picks up a holdall)* (**21**)

Jo Narr And ran away from God's call. *(Jo runs DSR and runs on the spot)*

(Chorus 2 and 3 form boat CS and Chorus 1 becomes sailor in boat) (**22**)

Narrator 2 Jo Narr . . .

Jo Narr Hey! *(To audience)* Was very, very happy to be going in the *opposite* direction. *(Jo tiptoes around the acting area, pays the 'sailor', gets in boat)* (**23**)

Narrator 1 Jo Narr embarked upon a boat, to cross the deep blue sea. *(Jo and Chorus 1 sway as if at sea)* He heaved a sigh of great relief. (**24**)

Jo Narr *(Relieved, wiping his brow)* Phew!

Narrator 2 And said . . .

Jo Narr *(Smugly)* God can't catch me! *(Shakes hands with the sailor)*

Narrator 2 But . . . *but*! (**25**)

Chorus 3 Came *thunder! (Moves DSR, Chorus 3 makes thunder movements. Jo, Chorus 1 and 3 sway violently. Chorus 2 thrown USL)* (**26**)

(17) This is lifted straight from pantomime style. Although it is not necessary to get the audience to join in, you can improvise and add a few more 'Oh nos', etc., but be careful not to hold up the momentum of the piece by overdoing it.

(18) Narrator must speak with authority, not amused, like a sarcastic teacher! The reaction from the rest annoyed to be cut short, and reluctantly obedient.

(19) Over-exaggerated action here. See other comments about 'Hey'.

(20) Often mime is a neglected art, and it is an art in itself. Although the holdall packing is swift, we must believe that there is a holdall there! Also the items put in should be recognisable in most cases. The actor should know exactly what he is doing, where it is coming from, weight, size, etc. Spend time working this out, let other members of the cast experiment and suggest things also. Be *constructively* critical and adjust accordingly.

(21) See (**20**). It's no use the holdall starting out large and ending up the size of a pea!

(22) (See *Quick Pics* in *Develop Your Skills*) It works well if the sailing boat is formed by the two Choruses sitting, feet apart, facing each other on the diagonal, leaving enough space for the 'sailor' to stand between the legs. To get the movement of the boat, they can sway backwards and forwards, or from side to side. Be prepared to try everyone's ideas until you find one that works best. Experiment.

(23) Jo puts finger to lips and *exaggeratedly,* Laurel and Hardy fashion, tiptoes around the acting area and mimes paying the 'sailor' and climbs into the boat.

(24) The sway works well, upstage first, then downstage, repeat again, continue until the Narrator says 'But', letting dialogue continue while the action goes on.

(25) This must be delivered with great presence, as the focus will be on the boat and the audience's eyes have to be torn away. So the narrator could use, voice alone, a move which catches the eye, *or* move from one side of the area to another. See which feels and works best. It is important to be well out of the way to observe the next action, which is quite hectic.

(26) How do you make thunder movements? Well . . . use imagination, experiment, think of the nature of thunder – rolling, loud, etc., and most of all make your movements big, but keep them well within the vicinity of Jo and the sailor, as their reaction will qualify the thunder movements. The remaining part of the boat can rock and be 'thrown' upstage, ready for the 'lightning' movement. The movement also needs to span only the words 'came *thunder*' which may have to be lengthened slightly to fit whatever you decide. It continues through to 'very, very sick'.

Chorus 2	And came lightning! *(Chorus 2 rushes at Jo)* (**27**)
All	The storm was fierce and frightening.
	(Jo and Chorus 1 tremble and mime rocking of 'boat') (**28**)
Narrator 1	Jo Narr . . .
Jo Narr	*(About to be sick)* Hey! *(Mimes puking over side of 'boat' CS)* (**29**)
Narrator 2	Was *very, very* sick! (**30**)
Chorus 1	Heavily polluting the deep blue sea! *(Jo curls up, hands together)* (**30**)
Narrator 1	Waves tumbled. *(Chorus 2 and 3 move either side of him)*
Chorus 2, 3	*(Actions of waves on either side of Jo Narr as they speak)* Tumble, tumble! (**31**)
Narrator 2	Sailors grumbled. *(Chorus 1 moves DSL)*
Chorus 1	*(Stamping feet)* Grumble, grumble. (**31**)
Narrator 1	*(Running across to DSR)* Waves *crashed!* *(Chorus 2 and 3 crash waves on both sides of Jo and Chorus 1 who react to the movement)* (**32**)
Narrator 2	Teeth gnashed!
Chorus 2, 3	*(Move towards audience gnashing teeth damatically)* Gnash! Gnash! (**33**)
Narrator 1	Lightning flashed!
Chorus 2, 3	Flash! Flash! (**34**)
Narrator 1, 2	Boat pitched. *(Pitching actions, all stagger SL)* Boat tossed. *(All stagger SR)* (**35**)
	(Jo reacts even though asleep) (**36**)
Chorus 1	Throw out the cargo *(All forwards)* or we're lost*! (All back. Chorus 1 throws out cargo)* (**37**)

(27) See above, but make sure that the moves are contrasting. The nature of lightning and the nature of thunder are very different, though closely related as a visual image.

(28) Throughout (**26**) and (**27**) storm movements on either side of the 'boat' as Jo and Chorus 1 shake with fear whilst continuing to mime the rocking of the 'boat'. Again movements must be large and any mime, such as hanging on to the mast, etc., needs to be well thought out.

(29) Accurate mime should make the audience identify with the feeling, and wince at the thought. In Jonah we all recognise so much of ourselves, and it's easier to take it on board through humour!

(30) These moves *must* be different from thunder and lightning. Crashing waves and spray, the boat movement must be synchronised, and this will help.

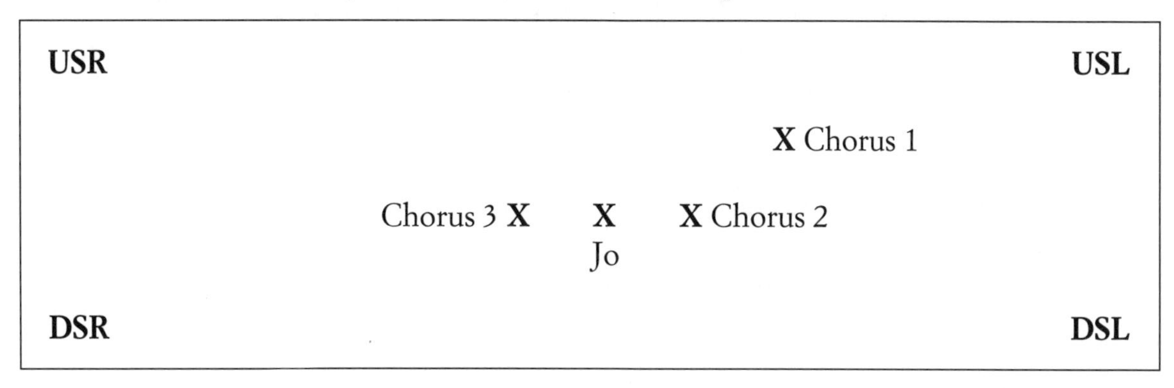

31) This word can sound so much like its meaning, so match meaning with expression and the right body language.

32) See note on thunder, lightning and waves. All must be larger than life, not just arms but the whole body and a personification of a stormy sea. Again action and reaction. It's no use having an amazing stormy sea effect if Jo and the sailor look as if they're sailing on a millpond!

33) Here we have another physical interpretation of *extremis;* make it larger than life, think of Popeye and the spinach syndrome!

34) See (**33**). One of Mustard Seed's interpretations was the 'flasher', that appeals to younger audiences, but is not suitable for services. It's a thought . . . make up your own mind!

35)(36) The pitching and tossing movements are represented by Chorus 1 as the sailor, slithering from one side of the deck to another, and by Jo who sleeps fitfully, while rolling back and forth. Don't allow the roll to get out of hand! It *has* been known. Keep it within a small space, or the actor might find himself on someone's knee!

37) Mime, though frantic and fast must not just be a general waving of arms! (For detailed work on Mime and Body Language see *Rock Solid – A foundation course in youth drama for worship.*) Keep the action going until Jo holds his nose and is about to jump.

Narrator 1 Jo Narr . . .

Jo Narr *(Jo yawns noisily, awakens and stands looking around in surprise)* Hey?

Narrator 1 Awoke from slumber, and heard the sailor's cry!

Chorus 1 Aaaaaaaaaaaaaaargh!

Jo Narr Oh Lord! Now I'm in lumber. *(Sags)* It's my fault if they die! (**38**) *(He kneels DSC with hands together, praying. Chorus 1, 2 and 3 line up one behind the other, making sea movements with their hands alternating)* (**39**)

Narrator He spoke to God and pleaded . . . God told him what was needed . . . So . . . Jo Narr . . .

Jo Narr *(Extremely miserable)* Hey! *(moving forward holding his nose as if to jump)*

Narrator Very, very unhappily jumped into the foaming brine. *(Jo jumps into 'sea')* (**40**)

Narrator The storm at once *abated. (Chorus hands forward in 'stop' action)* (**41**)

Narrator As Jo Narr sank below. *(Chorus move USC)*

Jo Narr *(Jo mimes sinking below the sea)* Glug, glug, glug. (**42**)

All Chorus *(Form fish shape US)* (**43**)

Narrator He gasped . . .

Jo Narr *(On his knees, agonised)* My days are ended, I'm going to die I know!

Narrator Then all at once . . . there came a *fish. ('Fish' moves forward, jaws snapping)* (**44**)

Narrator It gulped.

All Chorus Gulp. *('Fish' encircling Jo with joined arms)* (**45**)

(38) On 'Lord' fling arms up and look heavenwards, tense, yet still moving with the boat. Then sag, as the weight of worry hits you on 'It's my fault', and so on. We are not aiming for naturalism here!

(39) Cue 'die' and Jo sinks to his knees, once more in agonised prayer. While the Chorus move behind him, two kneeling but sitting back on heels and one kneeling upright, using hand and head movements to represent waves, at first wild, and gradually calming down.

(40) Jo jumps into the centre of the sea, and the chorus use arms to represent the splash.

(41) On the word 'abated' hands are stilled with palms facing the audience.

(42) Jo sinks down into foetal position, and the 'sea' rises and spins upstage ready to go into new grouping.

(43) Forms fish shape. Two side by side, facing each other, with both hands joined in the centre, so that they can make a 'jaws' action when they eventually move to Jo. For the moment they freeze, jaws open. The other chorus stands centrally behind them with one hand on each of their shoulders.

(44) Moving arms as jaws, move downstage to Jo who is frozen in horror.

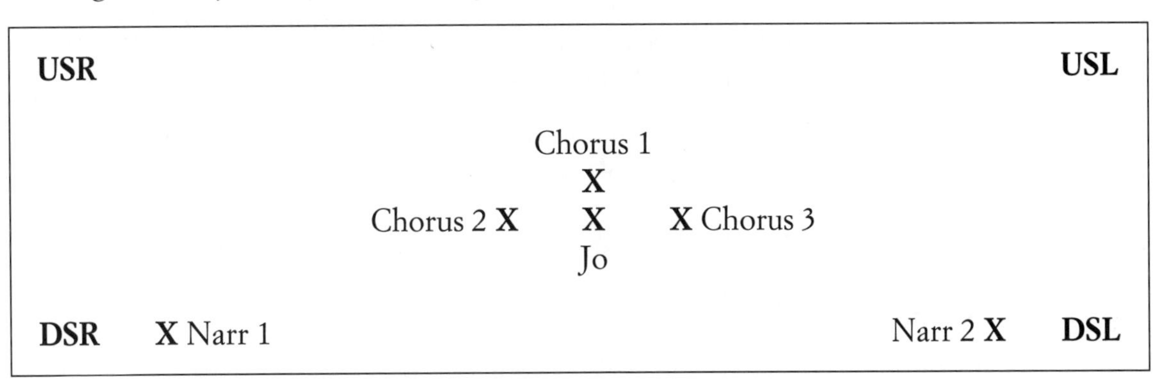

45) Encircle Jo with arms, as 'gulp' is spoken.

All Chorus	*My!* **Here's** a tasty dish! (**46**)
Narrator A	Mr Fish was very, very happy . . . to swallow Jo Narr **whole**, body and soul! Jo Narr quickly descended . . . (**47**)
Jo Narr	Descend, descend! *(Jo mimes struggle as 'fish' engulfs him)* (**48**)
Narrator	. . . Into the fish's guts . . . He thought . . .
Jo Narr	*(Struggling)* Is this a nightmare? Or am I going nuts? *(Jo kneels in prayer)* (**49**)
All Chorus	*(Smugly)* You're going nuts!
Narrator	He prayed to God his Father, and said . . .
Jo Narr	I'd really **rather** be very very miserable in **Blackpool**, than here in . . . **Wales!** (**50**)
Chorus 1	Fish thinks. (**51**)
Chorus 2	Joke stinks.
Narrator	Fish belches!
All Chorus	Burrrrrrrrp!
Narrator	Jo Narr squelches. *(Jo reels with the smell)* (**52**)
All Chorus	Squelch! Squelch!! (**53**)
Narrator	Belly rumbles.
All Chorus	Rumble. Rumble. *(Jo covers his ears)*
Narrator	Jo Narr tumbles. *(Jo falls flat on his face)*
All Chorus	Tumble. Tumble. (**54**)
Narrator	Fish coughed!

(46) Grin directly at audience and speak to them, emphasising bold words. This section is really corny, but as long as you involve the audience, they will collude with you and find the corny humour amusing. (I hope!)

(47) Jaws begin to close, as Jo struggles, popping out an arm or his head, etc., as the fight goes on.

(48) 'Descend, descend' is spoken with horrified expression during the course of the above struggle, and must begin after 'descended' immediately on cue.

(49) Freeze, with hands in prayer stretched above head and head looking upwards.

(50) Emphasise the bold words, but speaking it as if including the audience in the joke. A very short pause before 'Wales' allows them to anticipate the word, and then laugh in relief that they got it right!

(51) The Chorus reaction to the joke is to mirror what everybody feels, that it is the corniest joke they've heard in years! Nod in agreement on 'joke stinks'.

(52) Mischievous expression, as if to get their own back for the previous joke.

(53) Jo reels melodramatically. Chorus walk as if in wellie boots in mud, like children thoroughly enjoying themselves. Two steps in time with the words.

(54) Chorus 'tumble', i.e. totter in different directions, and come back to their starting position for 'fish coughed'.

All Chorus	Cough! Cough! *(Jo, on trying to get up, falls flat again)* (**55**)
Narrator	Fish sick!
All Chorus	Bueerrrrrrrrgh! (**56**)
Chorus 1	Spat out Jo Narr *(All Chorus spit as Jo falls forward, then into straight line. To audience)* (**57**)
Narrator	Mighty quick! *(Chorus form line and walk, hands in prayer, in circle, Jo follows)* (**58**) So Jo became a prophet.
All Chorus	*(Stop momentarily and turn heads to audience)* On Blackpool's golden mile.
	(All in line CS facing audience. Jo left of the line. Chorus take up various positions) (**59**)
Jo Narr	*(Looking at them with disgust)* I didn't like my job much!
Narrator	It took him quite a while to convince *all* in Blackpool! *(Chorus 1 kneels in prayer, looking saintly)* (**60**)
Jo Narr	That God's the only winner! *(Chorus 3 kneels in prayer, looking saintly)* (**60**)
Narrator	But he did. *(Chorus 2 kneels in prayer, looking saintly)* (**60**)
Jo Narr	*(To audience, wiping brow)* And was very, very pleased and hoped he'd never have to do it again!
Narrator	So when you visit Blackpool, and walk that mile of Gold, you must remember Jo Narr, who didn't do as he was told. *(Jo shakes head sadly, all Chorus wag fingers at him)* And if you hear God call you . . . *(hands to ears listening position)* (**61**)
All Chorus	*(Chorus, hands to mouths aiming at different parts of audience)* Yoooo-hoooooooo!
Narrator A	Don't let the thought appall you.

(55) Chorus cough in Jo's direction, timing it just as he is almost upright. It is most effective if he can fall forward with body rigid; if not, crumbling to a low level is almost as good dramatically.

(56) All lean forward as if being sick and hold the facial expressions momentarily before going into next section.

(57) Make spitting noises! Lean back, as if about to propel something with great force, then all in unison thrust forward. Jo must fall from the 'mouth' again, after trying to get up, and end up very close to the audience on a low level.

(58) On 'quick' the chorus as one become human, standing straight, hands together, walking in a tight circle ready for their next positions as sinners in Blackpool.

(59) Chorus in position of gambling, playing roulette, cheating, etc. Try to use different levels, and pay attention to body shape and facial expression, which should give the feeling of caricatured degenerates.

(60) Each move must be positive, kneel and hands together, turn and gaze heavenwards with hands together, kneel upright with hands stretched to heaven!

(61) Narrator must direct this speech confidentially to the audience, as if reporting on the coronation, or a very serious event.

All	For even Bingo players can be very, very repentant . . . *(pause) sometimes*! (**62**)
Jo Narr	*(Quizzically)* Hey! (**63**)
	(FREEZE)

(62) Choral speech. Unison, and clarity vital.

(63) The 'Hey' has to represent the feelings of someone who has had to face the truth and recognise it, with a kind of implicit warning to think before ignoring God's call. How? Experiment, and see what works best.

King Neb

An introduction

CHARACTERS

King Neb	*Shadrach/Chorus*	*Meschach/Chorus*
Abednego/Chorus	*Chorus A/Statue*	*Chorus B/Angel*

THEME Daniel 3

The story of Nebuchadnezzar, Daniel and the angels in the fiery furnace, with an emphasis on his worship of idols, Daniel's piety and the ultimate power of God to working miracles in seemingly impossible situations.

APPROACH

This sketch depends on an exaggerated style and tongue-in-cheek humour, yet has a serious message. It must be attacked with great gusto and enthusiasm, and the pace should be brisk. Rather like a moving 'cartoon', with all the elements of 'Tom and Jerry', and exaggerated body language that goes with this style.

Group work

Quick pics (10 min)

- Read the story of Shadrach, Meschach and Abednego (Daniel 3).
- Divide the group into threes or fours. Give them 15 seconds to create a visual image of some of the themes from the story. (Leader counts down the seconds.) On the count of fifteen the command FREEZE is given.
- Remind them about LEVELS. (See *Develop Your Skills*)

Discussion (10 min or longer if desired)

- Discuss the things which can often be the centre of our lives. Clothes, TV, car, bike, holidays, and so on.
- What are our idols? To what aspects of our natures do adverts appeal? Greed? Pride? Self-satisfaction? One-upmanship?

Group improvisation

Adverts (20 min)

- In the same groups as for Quick pics, create an advert to sell one of the following: a gold necklace, an extra large TV, a new brand of washing powder, a cream to make you younger, a car that never has to be cleaned.
- Try to create a jingle, and a good name for the product, and decide what part of our worldly nature it is to appeal to.
- Emphasise the need to keep it short, to use a good visual image at the beginning and to stress the name of the product and the marvellous things it will do for you. Suggest they take a well-known tune as a basis to write the jingle. Or use the format of a known advert, but change the name and the words. Stress exaggerated, larger-than-life statements, movements and facial expression. Remember voice projection and diction and 'body language'.

  Watch each advert and discuss the positives, then the ways of improvement. (See *Develop Your Skills* and *Rock Solid*.)

King Neb

(All standing in grotesque statue positions facing the audience US) (**1**)

King Neb *(SL)* I suppose you're wondering what we're doing? (**2**)

Chorus A *(CSL)* Can you guess?

Chorus B *(CS)* That's right!

Meschach *(CS)* We're being golden statues.

Shadrach *(CSR)* Do you know why?

Abednego *(SR)* Well . . . keep watching and we'll tell you.

King Neb Today's programme is about somebody *very* important.

Chorus A Do you know *who*? (**3**)

Shadrach Can you guess?

Meschach *(Patronisingly)* That's right!

Shadrach King Nebuchadnezzar!

Abednego Can *you* say Nebuchadnezzar? (**4**)

Abednego, Shadrach and Meschach *(Boasting) We* can. *(Move into boastful tableau)*

Others *(Despondently) We* can't *(Move into miserable tableau)* (**5**)

Chorus B *(To audience)* So for the sake of argument . . .

King Neb *(To audience)* We'll call him Neb, shall we?

All *(To audience)* KING NEB! (**6**)

Director's Tips

Starting positions

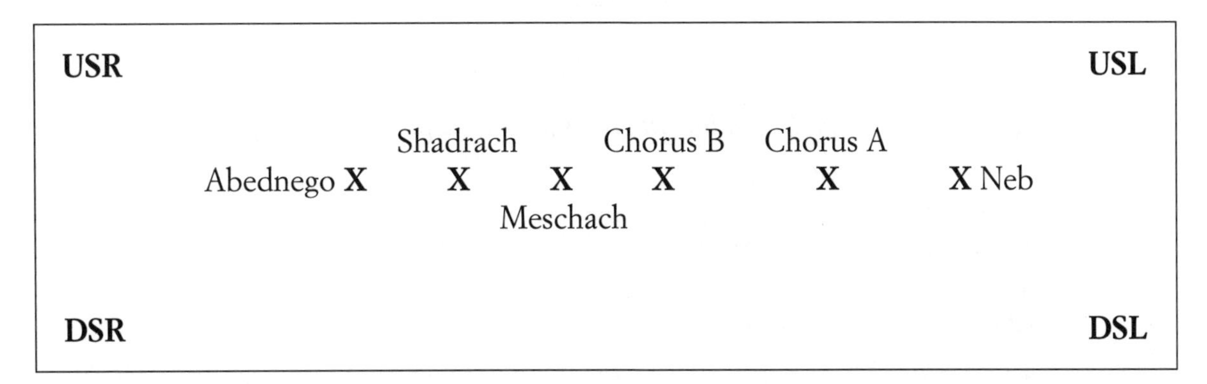

(1) These statues *must* be grotesque, including facial expressions. When the characters move into position they should walk to their places, then suddenly, and in unison, take up their poses. The audience should be amused at this point, thus setting the theme *(idols)* and the mood for the sketch.

(2) The sketch was devised in the style of a children's TV programme such as *Play Bus* or *Blue Peter*, so the emphasis in this section is as if speaking to very small children. Adult audiences find this quite funny, but small children will take it quite seriously!

(3) Slow down speech a little to make it even more patronising! When Shadrach says 'Nebuchadnezzar', it is with a *very* smug attitude.

(4) Spoken as a small child boasting about his/her achievements.

(5) Again exaggerated childish sulking, followed by the children's presenter attitude, taking the audience into their confidence, as if they are together in humouring these silly children! This sketch depends greatly upon the audience accepting the 'style' and going along with it. So, folks, everything must be larger than life here.

(6) Gleefully.

Abednego	*(Include audience)* What day is it today?
King Neb	It's *story* day! (**7**)
Shadrach	Which window shall we step through? (**8**)
Chorus A	Erm, Tina! *(To Shadrach)*
Shadrach	*(Cheerfully)* Yes, Georgina?
Chorus A	*(Confidentially)* Don't you think that's a *weeny* bit dangerous?
Shadrach	*(Puzzled)* What?
Chorus A	*(Politely exasperated)* Stepping through windows of course, Tina!
Shadrach	*(Irritated)* Let's go through the *door* then. *(Abednego and Neb form door)* (**9**)
Chorus A	OK.
Shadrach	*(Pushes Chorus B face-down on floor)* Follow me. *(Goes through 'door', steps over Chorus B, 'door' spins)* (**10**)
Meschach	Here we go! (**10**)
Chorus A	Won't be long now. (**10**)
King Neb	Are we ready? (**11**)
Chorus B	*(Gets up enthusiastically and trips and falls again. Neb and Abednego help Chorus B up. Neb stands CS.)* Come on then. Let's go!
Shadrach	*(To audience)* This is King Neb. *(Kneels DSC, back to audience)* (**12**)
Chorus B	*(To audience, moving SL)* This is the story of King Neb.
King Neb	*(CS)* Oh *smelly* . . . I'm bored!

(7) React excitedly to the idea of a story.

(8) Freeze in excited children statues after 'step through', until 'Let's go through the door then!' Chorus B and Shadrach exaggerate the over-the-top 'safety' angle, as is often done in children's programmes. Chorus B particularly talks down to Shadrach.

(9) Abednego and Neb should be central, facing the audience, at arm's length and stretching their hands out to touch fingers, rather like a saloon bar door in a Western! Chorus B excitedly hovers at the 'door'. Chorus B emerges here as the group 'clown', with all the clownish attributes, especially the one where people laugh at her expense.

(10) Shadrach is the bossy one, who likes to take the lead, and is totally unconcerned about pushing Chorus B out of the way and stepping on or over her. Shadrach pushes the arms of Neb and partner forwards, and they spin round full circle, before 'shutting' again. The others follow, each knocking down Chorus B who struggles to rise each time. As they run downstage towards the audience, they raise their arms, elbows bent, and shake their hands quickly, from side to side, in the air.

11) Neb sighs patiently here. As Chorus B stands, excited, steps forward, trips again and is helped up by the 'door' as her line 'come on then, let's go', is spoken as if everyone else is holding up proceedings. (Pace is so important here, this from (**9**)–(**11**) will need much rehearsal to get it spot on. Also it would be a good idea to check on, and possibly revise, stage falls at this point. See *King Neb* Introduction.)

12) Shadrach gestures to Neb CS, who stands with extremely sulky expression. Definitely a spoiled brat! Immediately after speaking, Shadrach kneels in front of Neb, with back to audience and gazes up at him adoringly.

Chorus A	*(Kneels SL on Neb's right)* What are we going to do today, King Neb? (**13**)
Meschach	*(Kneels SR on Neb's left)* Yes, tell us!
King Neb	*(Poses as 'The Thinker')* I'm thinking! (**14**)
Abednego	*(SR to audience, wisely)* He's thinking.
Meschach and Chorus A	*(Pose as 'The Thinker', still kneeling)* We're thinking.
Shadrach	*(Turning head to audience)* Are *you* thinking? (**15**)
King Neb	*(Excited)* I've thought. (**16**)
All	Phew!
King Neb	*(Excited)* Let's build a statue.
Chorus A	A golden statue. *(Chorus A becomes the statue)* (**17**)
Shadrach	*(Touching it)* Real gold.
King Neb	Let's worship it.
All	*(Excitedly enthusiastic, to new positions)* Yeah! *(Puzzled)* But why? (**18**)
King Neb	*(Falsely cheerful)* If you don't worship my statue . . . then I will throw you into the fiery furnace. You will fry . . . *(Hit Meschach)* (**19**)
Meschach	Ow! (**20**)
King Neb	And frizzle . . . *(Hit Abednego)* (**19**)
Abednego	Oh! (**20**)
King Neb	And spit . . . *(Hits Chorus B)* (**19**)
Chorus B	Oooh! (**20**)

(13) Chorus A skips to position and kneels, looking up adoringly.

(14) Neb does an extravagant, larger-than-life change of position, making 'The Thinker', fist clenched against forehead, eyes closed, etc. As the others echo his words, they imitate his position, though remaining on their knees.

(15) Shadrach twists to look at audience in the manner of 'Your country needs you' Kitchener, and delivers the line in an authoritative way, with great emphasis on the *you.* In a way this identifies the audience with Neb, and indirectly gets them to think about their attitudes towards the material things of life. Well . . . that's the idea anyway!

(16) Again a swift change of mood, conveyed as much by body language as by tone of voice. (See *Rock Solid, Direct Approach Book One,* and *Develop Your Skills* – particularly voice warm-ups and body language.) Neb moves SR.

(17) Chorus A moves into the centre and freezes as statue, with a self-satisfied expression – the stance of a definite 'poser'.

(18) The contrast between the forced excitement of 'Yeah', as they run to new positions, and the rather whining 'But why', can be emphasised by a short pause, and a sudden change of body language before 'But why'. The statue becomes a follower again and Neb moves into the centre of the kneeling group.

19) We found King Neb's next speeches to be most effective when they started in a false cheerful way and ended in violent hysterics. Hit, i.e. tap on the head, on the cues, smiling sweetly as he does this.

20) The other characters each react differently to the attack, using a different vowel sound in polite protest.

King Neb	And sizzle *(Hits Shadrach)* (**19**)
Shadrach	Agh! (**20**)
King Neb	Until you *die!* (**21**)
All	Er . . . OK, you win! *(They bow to statue frantically)* (**22**)
Meschach	Oooh! Rhubarb and custard! (**23**)
Abednego	Ooooooh! Calor Gas heater.
Chorus B	Oooh! I'll have a shandy, I'll have a beer!
Shadrach	Oooh! Boil in the bag chicken!
All	*(Repeat their lines together, twice)*
Chorus A	*(To audience)* However . . . (**24**)
All	However! *(All move into line US)* (**25**) *(Singing)* By the **ri**vers of **Babylon** there **were** three **men**, (**26**) And **they** were **called** Shadrach, **Mes**chach and A**bed**nego.

Shadrach My name is Shadrach.
All His name is Shadrach.
Shadrach And I'm a plumber.
All Yes, he's a plumber.
Shadrach This is my plunger.
All That is his plunger.
Shadrach And I worship God.
All And he worships God.

Meschach My name is Meschach. (**27**)
All His name is Meschach.
Meschach And I'm a baker.
All And he's a baker.
Meschach And I bake cakes.
All And he bakes cakes.
Meschach And I worship God.
All And he worships God.

(21) Climax of Neb's violent displeasure, *must* have a cringe reaction from his followers.

(22) Bow cartoon style, waving arms frantically.

(23) The following speeches are preceded by a lengthened Ooooh sound, and are delivered in fear of the great king, hands raised above head as speech is delivered and then bowing to the ground. All in unison. Don't gabble. Keep up the pace. Jump in on cues VERY fast. After each individual line has been spoken, let yourselves go wild as you repeat your lines twice, together! Finish exactly together.

(24) All come up from bow with Chorus A. Neb stands, arms folded, looking smug.

(25) All kneel up immediately as this line is said, then extremely quickly they all move into a line US, Neb SR, Abednego CSR, Chorus A CS, Meschach CS, Chorus B CSL, Shadrach SL. They turn to the Right but with faces towards the audience as they sing to the tune of 'Rivers of Babylon', another connection with idols!)

(26) The song is unaccompanied and sounds good when it is sung raucously and enthusiastically. Good diction, energetic, well-timed moves performed in unison. All the imitation must be accurate. A good idea is to practise in a circle, before trying to work from memory. This will require plenty of concentration in rehearsal to get it slick!

By the **ri**vers of **Baby** **lon** (beat) there **were** three **men**
(kick) (kick) (kick), (kick) (Turn front, hands on knees)

And **they** were **called** Shadrach, **Me**schach and A**bed**nego
(sway right)(sway left) (Turn around as below except Shadrach, Meschach, Abednego, who run forward, as others turn on spot shaking hands in the air, 'rock 'n' roll' style.

(Shadrach holds plunger in air. Meschach stirs in a bowl, Abednego counts money.)

Shadrach **My name is Shadrach** *(Swings hips)*
All His name is Shadrach *(Imitate Shadrach)*
Shadrach And I'm a **plum**ber *(Thumb to chest)*
All Yes, he's a plumber *(Imitate Shadrach)*
Shadrach This is my **plung**er *(Holds up imaginary plunger)*
All That is his **plung**er *(As Shadrach)*
Shadrach And I worship God *(To audience)*
All And he worships God *(All turn on spot waving hands in air)*

(27) **Meschach** My **name** is **Me**schach *(Thumbs in imaginary braces. Knees bend twice)*
All His name is Meschach *(All imitate Meschach)*
Meschach And I'm a **baker** *(Large basin cradled in L arm, stir with spoon)*
All And he's a baker *(As Meschach)*
Meschach And I bake cakes *(Rub stomach)*
All And he bakes cakes *(Rub stomach)*
Meschach And I worship God *(To audience)*
All And he worships God *(All turn on spot waving hands in air)*

Abednego My name is Bendy. (**28**)
All His name is Bendy.
Abednego And I'm a banker.
All Yes, he's a banker.
Abednego I own a bank.
All He owns a bank.
Abednego And I worship God.
All And he worships God.
We worship God. We worship God. (**29**)
We don't rate Idols. We worship God. Yeah! (**30**)

Chorus B King Neb was very angry . . . He *flew* into a rage. (**31**)

King Neb Aaaaaaaaaaaaaaaaargh! *(Screaming around angrily, and stamping feet as if in a tantrum. Chorus A and B DSL, Shadrach, Meschach, Abednego DSR, diagonal line)* (**32**)

Chorus B And ordered the three men to appear before him. (**33**)

King Neb Worship my statue. (**34**)

Shadrach *(Firmly)* No. (**35**)

King Neb Worship my statue.

Meschach *(Patiently firm)* No.

King Neb Worship my statue.

Abednego *(Determined)* No.

King Neb *Why not?* (**36**)

Shadrach Because . . . (**37**)

Meschach *(To audience boldly)* **Our** God.

Abednego *(To audience boldly)* Is **greater**.

All three *(To audience boldly)* Than **your** God.

King Neb *(Angrily)* Open the doors of the fiery furnace. (**38**)

(**28**) **Abednego** My name is Bendy *(Hands outstretched to audience)*
All His name is Bendy *(As Abednego)*
Abednego And I'm a banker *(Counts money on his hand)*
All Yes, he's a banker *(As Bendy)*
Abednego I own a bank *(Both arms circular expansive movement)*
All He owns a bank *(As Bendy)*
All And he worships God *(All turn on spot waving hands in air)*

(**29**) **All** We worship God. We worship God *(All wildly freak out to the rhythm)*
We don't rate Idols. We worship **God** *(Stop on God)*

(**30**) (Clap) **Yeah!** (All gesture towards Neb, who has watched with mounting fury.)

(**31**) Chorus B runs DSL with urgency to confide the latest news of Neb to the audience, while Neb looks as if he is about to burst. Chorus A moves DSL as Neb rages.

(**32**) Neb flies around like a balloon with the air forced out of it, screaming. Everyone cowers out of his way. Shadrach, Meschach and Abednego crouch DSR

(**33**) Shadrach, Meschach and Abednego form a diagonal line SL, Neb CS, Chorus A and B are DSR.

(**34**)(**35**)With great authority, as if expecting to be obeyed. The 'no' speeches must be equally firm, and *very* calm to contrast again with Neb's mounting anger as he goes once again into 'spoiled brat' mode. Remember, the contrast is really between those who are moving in God's strength with an unshakable faith, and a man whose life depends on material things, and his own whims!

(**36**)(**37**)Build up Neb's petulant anger and scream this speech, in the way a child does when thwarted. If you're feeling adventurous, and not too hoarse by now, you could throw in a stamp or two! These speeches must carry conviction. Suddenly it's serious! They know that to criticise Neb is to court certain death, but as one, they defend their God.

(**38**) Chorus A and B form the doors of the fiery furnace DSL on a diagonal. This is important.

Chorus B, A	Creak! (**39**)
Chorus A	One. *(Shadrach goes through doors)* (**40**)
Shadrach	Agh! *(Horrified)*
Chorus B	Two. *(Meschach goes through doors)* (**41**)
Meschach	*(As if burning hot)* Ow!
Chorus A	Three! *(Abednego goes through doors)* (**42**)
Abednego:	*(Tearfully)* Oooh! *(Chorus B moves USC in neutral with back to audience)* (**43**)
Chorus A	How many men did Neb put into the fiery furnace? Let's count them, shall we?
Chorus A	One . . . *(Shadrach DSC waves to audience)* (**44**) Two . . . *(Meschach DSC waves to audience)* Three . . . *(Abednego DSC waves to audience)* But don't despair.
Chorus B	*(Becomes angel in centre of circle)* God sent his angel. (**45**)
Chorus A	To protect them from the flames. There are really four men there, not three! As the flames burned higher, out they came from the burning fire. Not even burnt by a single flame! (**46**)
King Neb	One. *(Shadrach jumps out and freezes)* (**47**)
Chorus A	Two. *(Meschach jumps out and freezes)*
King Neb	Three. *(Abednego jumps out and freezes)*
Shadrach	Shadrach. (**48**)
Meschach	Meschach.
Abednego	Abednego.
King Neb	*(Singing)* Your God is great. (**49**)
All	Our God is great.

(39) Doors open outwards, quite slowly, with a 'haunted house'-type creak.

(40) On cue 'one', still in 'door' position, Chorus A and B go into cartoon 'thought' position, silly 'I've got an idea' grin and 'door' arm bent with finger pointing upwards. Shadrach moves to door, pauses before entering. Chorus A and B slap Shadrach's behind, which he covers with his hands. A short, pained look towards audience before running, knees raised, into furnace. Meschach watches thoughtfully. As Shadrach runs, Meschach imitates 'door', gets idea, 'thought' position.

(41) Cue 'two' and Meschach covers behind with hands, smiles smugly at audience as he runs, knees high, to the 'door'. Pauses as 'door' repeats the 'thought' action as before. Simultaneously clout him on the head. Meschach looks at audience with pained expression, clutches head, and enters, joining Shadrach who walks in a circle, hands in prayer, and peaceful expression. Meschach does the same.

(42) Abednego watches thoughtfully. As Meshach runs into the furnace Abednego goes into 'thought' position. Cue 'three': Abednego covers head with hands, smiles smugly at audience as he runs to the 'door'. Pauses as Chorus A and B repeat 'thought' action, exchange looks, and simultaneously knee him on the behind. Abednego looks at audience with pained expression, clutches his behind and enters furnace joining the others in the circle, hands in prayer, peaceful expressions.

(43) It is important that Chorus B does not move in a way which will take away the focus from the action. USR and across the back slowly in NEUTRAL. Once in position total stillness is required.

(44) Chorus A as children's presenter, remaining DSR, talking to audience as if they are children. The three men in turn must time their circle so that they are DSC on the following cues: One = Shadrach; Two = Meschach; Three = Abednego. When they reach DSC front they turn to audience with wide grin, both hands in 'stick 'em up' position, turning wrists quickly from side to side. A grin, then immediate change to serious expression, hands together as they resume the circle. This is only a momentary pause, as they continue walking all the time. Neb reacts smugly. DSR.

(45) As Chorus speaks, Chorus B turns and moves to centre of circle, raising hands high, palms outwards as a priestly blessing, and becomes the angel, speaking as the angel.

(46) Spoken dramatically with emphasis on the underlined words. Neb begins to look anxious, and focuses on the furnace with an extremely worried expression.

(47) If the circle is kept going (in a clockwise direction), and timed well, then the characters should be coming to the front on the appropriate number. On the word, they jump forward, grinning happily and waving hands as before. Shadrach jumps CSL, Meschach jumps CS and Abednego CSR. They freeze at the point of greatest energy. (See *Focus Freeze* in *Develop Your Skills*.) Neb changes position on each number, each position an expression of horror and amazement.

(48) As they speak their names, each character 'stick 'em up' arms position, hands waving, turn on the spot with knees high and jolly expression, freezing as they reach the front.

(49) Sings with wild abandon!

King Neb	For he saved you. *(Point at them)*
All	For he'll save *you. (Point at Neb)*
King Neb	I am a king.
All	You are a king.
King Neb	But I can worship him too.
All	You can worship him to-ooo! (**50**) You can worship him to-ooo. You can worship him too. For he'll save you. YEAH!
	(FREEZE) (**51**)

(**50**) See (**29**).

(**51**) All freeze in tableau, ending positions worked out previously, with focus on Neb, hands together, serious expression, gazing heavenwards, the others grouped around, having made a final big gesture on 'Yeah! Hold the position for two to three seconds. (See *Quick Pics* in *Develop Your Skills*.)

Rock Solid

An introduction

CHARACTERS

Sinky *Rocky* *Chorus 1* *Chorus 2* *Chorus 3*

THEME Luke 6:47-49; Matthew 7:24-27

This sketch is based on the parable of the two builders, and is set in modern times. Success is built on using God's master plan and not on making one up to suit ourselves!

APPROACH

This sketch is similar in approach to both King Neb and Noah, as it uses stylised movement and song-and-dance style as its basis. It is best performed after concentrated rehearsal, as it will fall flat if the moves are not well timed and slick. It gets over the point through humour, and requires pace and attack.

Develop some style: song and dance (1 hour or longer if desired)

- In groups of three or four, improvise one of the following fairy stories, in Song and Dance: Red Riding Hood; Cinderella; Jack and the Beanstalk; Babes in the Wood; Sleeping Beauty.
- Stage it as a cabaret, or musical, including dance steps, and (often rather corny) synchronised moves. It is useful to '**Storyboard**' the themes first. (See *Jo Narr* – Introduction, and *Glossary* – Song and Dance.) Giving them the main points of the stories on a card each saves time, and reminds them of details of the stories.
- Using the tune of a song or nursery rhyme with a simple tune, rewrite the words to fit your story. For example, the beginning of the 'Light under the bushel' story using 'Oh My Darling Clementine':
  Keep your light upon the lamp stand
  do not hide it 'neath the bed,
  for a light upon the lamp stand
  bright and glowing beams will shed . . . (Here's one for you to finish!)

  It would be handy to have pencils and paper for the groups to scribble on. You will find that some groups automatically reach for pencil and paper. Let them use it to jot down ideas, but get them on their feet trying things out. Try to persuade them not to sit and write the whole script, but to put it into action section by section.

  You never know, the muse might take them, and several good original ideas could come out of it. If you're really enthusiastic, then give them parables and Bible stories, after they have practised on the fairy stories. This could lead to a series of workshops, if you feel ready for the challenge!

  Be positive if the groups haven't finished, or if they only have a rough outline. Stress that you are meeting not only to learn drama skills, but to find out more about God's word, and that all offerings in this context are valuable. Everyone can learn from everyone else in all areas. All improvisations, in whatever style, take time. Don't worry if they clutch rough scripts when they present their ideas.

  Watch each scene together, discuss positively. Never put anyone down. Build on the good things, and encourage improvement. Maybe you've got something good, that's ready to be scripted?

Rock Solid

(Parable of the two builders – Luke 6:47-49; Matthew 7:24-27)

(Sinky stands SL. Rocky SR. Chorus 1, 2 and 3 positioned USC. All have backs to audience) (**1**)

Sinky	*(Turns)* Hey up! Hello! I'm Sinky Sand. *(Waves)* I'm pleased to meet you all. *(Looks around)* It's nice out here, the weather's grand. (**2**)
All Chorus	*(Turning and speaking over their left shoulder)* And the view's not bad an' all! *(Turn with backs to audience)* (**3**)
Sinky	*(To audience)* Be just right spot to build an 'ouse if I were so inclined. But I'm that busy doing nowt, I just can't find the time! *(Freeze)* (**4**)
Chorus 1	*(Turns)* One, two, three! *(Chorus 2 turns on 'two', Chorus 3 turns on 'three')* (**5**)
All Chorus	*(Singing to the tune of 'Mr Sandman')* Hey, Mr Sandman, build us a **farm,** *(dance step forward)* with a fitted **kitch**en *(All Chorus, hands on hips, RH raised, swing hips)* and a **burgl**ar al**arm**! *(All cross right arm, then left across chest)* (**6**)
Chorus 1	*(Spoken)* Make it luxurious! (**7**)
Chorus 2	With a swimming pool.
Chorus 3	*(Ecstatically)* And an en suite bathroom. *(Chorus 1 and 3 kneel)*
Chorus 1, 3	And a bright green loo.
Chorus 2	*(Flushing movement moving DSC)* Ssssshhhhhhhh!
Chorus 1	*(Singing and moving DSCR)* Na na na na na! (**8**)
Rocky	*(Turning and gyrating hips to the rhythm of the tune)* My name's hard (**9**)

Director's Tips

Starting positions

USR			**USL**
	Chorus 1 **X** **X** **X** Chorus 3		
	Chorus 2		
X Sinky		Rocky **X**	
DSR			**DSL**

(1) All characters in position, in NEUTRAL (see *Glossary),* backs to audience.

(2) An accent is effective for this character, Cornish, Norfolk, Welsh or the local accent. It is important that he is a harmless character, really rather nice, just a bit daft sometimes, then the audience can react well with him, and identify, as we're all inclined to build on unsure foundations at times, just like him. It's easier to be a Sinky than a Rocky. Know what I mean? He needs to make instant friendly rapport with the audience. Eye contact, conversational tone, etc., all helps.

(3) The Chorus are like a backing group, they echo the action, provide interest, and fill in the blank bits. They portray human and non-human attitudes and emotions. Essentially fickle, but full of life, energy and attraction, better played by girls, or boys in drag perhaps! (Of course you could reverse the roles all together and have female Rocky and Sinky!) It is very important that all their actions are in unison when together, and larger than life when alone. When they turn and look over their shoulders they must all be together for maximum impact.

(4) Appreciative look around, shrug shoulders and talk confidentially to audience, assuming their sympathy.

(5) Sharp turns on each number, all turning with the same shoulder first, it looks better.

(6) Synchronised movement and clear diction vital, so that the audience focuses on the words communicated and not one person. Madonna is a good role model for the type of movement which could be used!

(7) The following lines must be over-emphasised with appropriate movement, like an advert for perfume, or luscious chocolate (see *King Neb* – Introduction, 'Adverts').

(8) This is sung with the rhythm of a blues riff, e.g. Na **na** na na **na** 1 – 2, etc. It is a motif which is repeated many times in the sketch, often with repetitive movements. It is important, therefore, that the movement is slick and synchronised, and focuses on the immediate action, complementing it, without distracting from it. The rhythm must be kept up between Rocky's speeches and the chorus movement and song. Keep the pace going.

(9) Expansive gesture on the word 'hard'. Sinky yawns, makes himself comfortable, and watches, shaking head occasionally, obviously thinks Rocky is a fool.

Chorus 2 *(Singing and moving DSC to Chorus 1)* Na na na na na!

Rocky But you can call me Rock.

Chorus 3 *(Singing and moving DSC to Chorus 2)* Na na na na na!

Rocky No time to talk right now.

All Chorus Na na na na na!

Rocky My schedule's non-stop!

All Chorus *(Turning towards Rocky)* Na na na na na!

Rocky I'm building a house on this slab of granite. (**10**)

All Chorus Na na na na na! *(Chorus 1 moves to left of Rocky and poses)* (**11**)

Rocky When this house is finished.

All Chorus Na na na na na! *(Chorus 2 moves looking over Rocky's shoulder and poses)*

Rocky It'll be the best on the planet!

All Chorus Na na na na na! *(Chorus 3 moves to R of Rocky and poses)*

Rocky I'm a dude.

All Chorus Na na na na na!

Rocky Resident of Bude. (**12**)

All Chorus Na na na na na!

Rocky I'm no fool . . . I'm *cool!* (**13**)

All Chorus *(Scream and grab him as if he's a pop star, then freeze)*

Sinky *(Moves SL to frozen group)* He's not cool *(Chorus come to life and listen)* . . . That bloke's a fool. *(Moves away DSR)* (**14**)

(**10**) Expansive gesture to indicate slab of granite.

(**11**) Each move by the chorus is in the 'model' culture, very 'posed' and artificial, treating Rocky as a famous star. Shades of Tom Cruise here, I think! Or Matt Dillon. Quick Pics could be developed by the group. (See *Develop Your Skills.*)

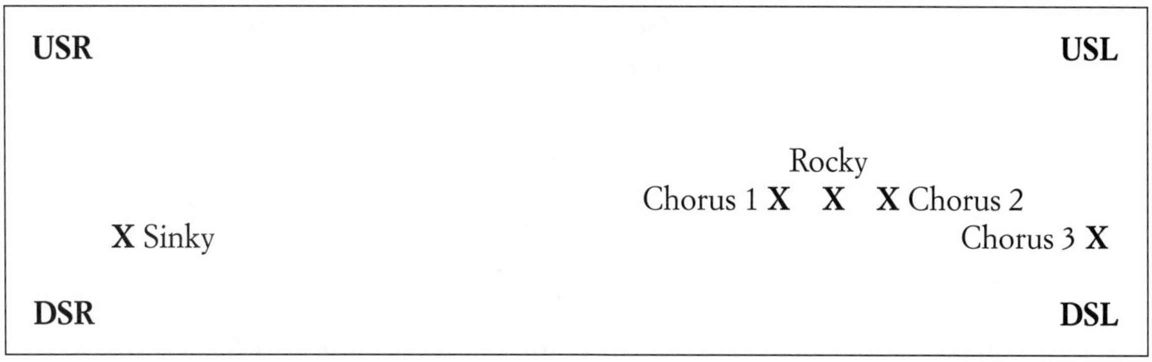

USR		**USL**
	Rocky	
	Chorus 1 **X** **X** **X** Chorus 2	
X Sinky		Chorus 3 **X**
DSR		**DSL**

(**12**) Why Bude, you ask? Well, quite a number of people there were instrumental in supporting Mustard Seed, and this sketch was written for them! A kind of 'thank you' for all those pies and pasties, counselling and love given to us during our times with them. But you can change the venue if you wish. It's the message that's important.

13) 'Cool' pose frozen, like a still Levi's advert! The girls scream and drape themselves around him like adoring fans in frozen tableau. Sinky stands as they scream.

14) To audience and Chorus, with a slight laugh in his voice. As he speaks, the Chorus turn heads sharply to look at Sinky, easily swayed. They transfer affections to Sinky who obviously approves, and feels he has won a victory. Rocky remains frozen.

Chorus 1 *(Moves to Sinky)* His house will be a mess!

Chorus 3 *(To R of Sinky, arm round his shoulder)* When you build yours . . . beside the sea.

Sinky *(Smugly)* It'll take half the time!

Chorus 2 *(Smugly, to audience)* And cost *far* less. *(Chorus grouped adoringly around Sinky)* (**15**)

Sinky Ooh! *(Thrilled)* Come on then, give us a hand! *(Kneels, miming wall building)* (**16**)

Sinky Splosh slap. Splosh slap.

(All speaking together)

Sinky Splosh slap. Splosh slap
Chorus 2 Chop! Chop! Chop!
Chorus 3 Dig. Dig. Dig.
Chorus 1 Build. Build. Build.

Rocky *(CS to Sinky)* Excuse me, sir? I don't think you grasp the geological properties of sand. (**17**)

All Chorus *(Gormlessly)* Eh?

Sinky *(Defensively)* I do! And these girls are givin' me an 'and. *(Gestures to Chorus)* (**18**)

(Rocky moves DSL and carefully measures, checks, and begins to build) (**19**)

(All together as before)

Chorus 2 Chop! Chop! Chop!
Chorus 3 Dig. Dig. Dig.
Chorus 1 Build. Build. Build
Sinky Splosh slap. Splosh slap.

Chorus 2 Finished. (**20**)

Chorus 3 Finished.

Chorus 1 Finished.

(**15**) Freeze for a second in admiring tableau, draped around Sinky, who looks smug.

(**16**) 'Ooh' is spoken at the end of the freeze, and then Sinky kneels, miming building a wall in a slapdash fashion. The chorus remains frozen, exactly in the same position, until he asks for help, they rush to new 'building' positions. It is a useful idea for Sinky to say his line once before the chorus join in, to get the rhythm going (see *Rock Solid* – Surveying the Ground, 'Essence Machines'). Rocky watches their slapdash work sadly.

(**17**) He moves to the group. On 'excuse me' they stop as one and stare at him. As he finishes, jaws drop and the 'eh?' is delivered in unison, gormlessly. You could try irritated, and see which works best for you.

(**18**) 'I do' is very defensive, and the rest of the line is spoken boastfully, with the emphasis on 'me'.

(**19**) Simultaneously Rocky turns away and meticulously measures his patch of ground, tests the soil, digs foundations and builds carefully, as the others continue as before. You will have to judge the number of times that Sinky and co repeat their actions, to give Rocky time to show a contrast in attitude. The emphasis is on attitude. And it's the way the job is tackled which is important, not completing the mime in the exact time it takes. Economy of movement and precision for Rocky; careless, wild and lazy for the others.

(**20**) 'Finished' should be a bit like a verbal Mexican wave, with a little overlap of the end of each word. And as each one says the word, move into frozen 'self-satisfied' tableau, with the focus on Sinky who sits or leans back lazily, surrounded by admirers yet again!

Sinky Finished.

All Chorus Finished. *(All freeze in admiring position)*

Sinky *(Kneeling)* My house is finished first of all, it's fit for queen and king! The dude's still working dawn till dusk, when we're all partying. *(Wild party actions)* (**21**)

All Chorus *(Chorus dance the 'sand dance' around Sinky with vocal sound effects!)* Nyow Nyow **Nyow Nyow Nyow!** Nyow Nyow **Nyow** Nyow **Nyow** Nyow **Nyow**. (**22**)

Rocky *(Stepping forward commandingly)* STOP! (**23**)

Chorus 1 Na **na** na na **na**! *(To CS, hips swinging)* (**24**)

Rocky *(DSR)* **Two** years **lat**er.

Chorus 2 Na **na** na na **na**! *(To CS, hips swinging)*

Rocky **My** task's complete.

Chorus 3 Na na na na na! *(To CS hips swinging)*

Rocky That **hard** work took its **toll**

All Chorus Na na na na na!

Rocky But never **mind** we're safe and **sound** . . .

All Chorus Na na na na na!

Rocky So **let's** all **rock.** (**25**)

All Chorus And **roll**. *(Freeze momentarily)* (**26**)

(Chorus 2 and 3 dance CS singing to the tune of 'Rock Around the Clock'; Chorus 1 dances with Rocky DSL) (**27**)

We're gonna rock around your house tonight!
We're gonna rock rock rock till broad daylight.
We're gonna rock rock rock around your house tonight!

(21) It is quite effective if 'partying' is really wild and loud, acting as an action activator for the chorus who go into 'sand dance' actions round and round Sinky (see **22**).

(22) Now what's a sand dance? Well . . . you step forward on the right foot and bring the left foot to the right. At the same time, the right arm is bent at right angles, with the hand making another right angle, and the left arm pointing, palm upwards, behind the back! As the step is taken by the right foot, the right arm stretches forward, and as the left foot is brought to the right, the arm bends again. The left hand does as near that as possible – backwards. If you have understood all that, you're a genius, and can add the chin moving forward and back at the same time as the arms. When you've added the vocals . . . it's easy! Now pick yourself off the floor, and if you can't do it still, find someone over 50 and ask them to demonstrate for you!

(23) Rocky must rescue the Chorus from their dance, by coming in on cue quickly, with a commanding tone, and a big arm and hand gesture.

(24) Remember that the Chorus are a backing group (see **3**). Sing (see *Glossary*) with the rhythm of a blues riff as before, e.g. Na **na** na na **na** 1 – 2, etc. It is a motif which is repeated many times in the sketch, often with repetitive movements. It is still important, therefore, that the movement is slick and synchronised, and focuses on the immediate action, without distracting. It is there to complement the action, not to take it over! The rhythm must be kept up between Rocky's speeches and the chorus movement and song. They keep the pace up. Rocky is the difficult part to play in this sketch, because he's the 'good guy', and can come over a bit smug if you are not careful. He should also be an attractive personality, but strong, trendy and definite. This is helped by the chorus rhythm which should be continued by Rocky in his speeches and movement. Rocky's movement should be very strong!

(25) On 'Rock' change position into a rock dance pose, feet apart, hand in the air, and freeze.

(26) On 'Roll', the chorus go into a rock tableau and freeze. Sinky sits in his house, eating, smoking, drinking, and ignoring the rest.

(27) Energetic dance here in rock 'n' roll style. Singing at the same time of course. Make sure that you plan all the moves, so that everyone knows exactly what to do. Usually the cast will be able to create their own, which is much better than giving them every single move.

We're gonna rock around your house tonight!
We're gonna rock rock rock till broad daylight
We're gonna rock gonna rock around your house tonight.
YEAH! *(Party tableau)* (**28**)

Chorus 1 *(CS)* Stop! (**29**)

Chorus 2 *(To Chorus 1)* Wait!

Chorus 1 *(To Chorus 2)* Hang on a minute!

Chorus 2 Did I hear the rain? (**30**)

Chorus 1 Did I hear the wind?

Chorus 2 Did I hear thunder roll and lightning crash? *(Sink and Rock exchange looks, then at the Chorus)*

Sinky *(Horrified)* No! *(Chorus move around Sinky making weather noises)* (**31**) *and* (**32**)

(On knees) The wind is whistling through the walls. Rain is pouring through me ceiling. *(To audience)* My house is crumbling round my ears . . . I have this dreadful feeling! Maybe I should have planned it more, perhaps I was too slapdash? Perhaps the dude was talking sense when he said my house would . . . (**33**)

Chorus 1 Creeeeeak! *(Leaning* in*)* (**34**)

Chorus 2 Creeeeeak! *(Leaning in)*

Chorus 3 Creeeeeak! *(Leaning in)*

All Chorus Crash! *(Land on top of him)* (**35**)

Rocky Poor old Sinky.

Chorus 1 *(Stand)* Na na na na na! (**36**)

Rocky *(To audience)* But he was warned.

Chorus 2 *(Stand)* Na na na na na!

(28) On 'Yeah', a frozen party tableau. Before working out the sequence in (**27**), It's a good idea to make this tableau, so that the cast know exactly where they must finish after the dance.

(29) The next three speeches must be extremely melodramatic, with larger-than-life gestures.

(30) Rocky and Sinky look first at the Chorus, then at the audience, then at each other. Time this exactly. Rocky is unperturbed, but Sinky's expressions must become more and more panic stricken.

(31) Hands to head, totally horrified tone.

(32) Chorus move threateningly around Sinky making weather noises: Chorus 1 = rain; Chorus 2 = wind; Chorus 3 = thunder and lightning. Big actions accompany the sounds, and personify the elements. Sinky is forced to his knees in desperation, while Rocky mimes opening his door, putting out a hand to feel the rain, shivering, closing his door and reading a book.

(33) This speech is very much addressed to the audience, in an effort to gain sympathy.

(34) By this time the chorus should be standing one behind, and one on either side of Sinky, who is on the floor, cowering and covering his ears. On each elongated 'creeeeeak' all the Chorus sway and lean drunkenly. Leaning further on each creak!

(35) Landing on top of someone sounds easy, but, believe me, it can be dangerous unless it is worked out carefully beforehand so that no one gets hurt! There's always one person who gets carried away! Don't let them, or they'll be carried in the direction of the hospital! Protect Sinky at all costs! (See *Noah's Rainbow* – Introduction, 'Stage falls'.)

(36) See (**24**).

Rocky	*(Shaking head sadly)* He knew the consequences.
All Chorus	*(Stand)* Na na na na na!
Rocky	Of building houses on sand.
All Chorus	*(CS)* Na na na na na! (**37**)
Rocky	Which offers no defences.
All Chorus	*(CS)* Na na na na na!
Rocky	So if you've got a task to do.
All Chorus	*(Chorus 1 to Rocky)* Na na na na na! *(Freeze)* (**38**)
Rocky	Take care and do it well.
All Chorus	*(Chorus 2 to Rocky)* Na na na na na! *(Freeze)*
Rocky	And when the storms of life appear.
All Chorus	*(Chorus 2 to Rocky)* Na na na na na! *(Freeze)*
Rocky	You'll live . . . your tale to tell . . . So remember – don't mock.
All Chorus	*(Change position)* Na na na na na! (**39**)
Rocky	Those who work round the clock!
All Chorus	*(Change position)* Na na na na na!
Rocky	And build your house *strong!* On *God (pause)*. The *Rock!* (**40**)
All Chorus	*(Change position)* YEAH! (**41**)

(37) Turn mockingly to Sinky, who struggles up to look at them in complete misery.

(38) Each move by the chorus is in the 'model' culture, very 'posed' and artificial, treating Rocky as a famous star.

(39) Change tableau; make sure all move together with definite move and freeze, looking adoringly at Rocky.

(40) Directly to the audience. After 'God', look swiftly to the right and back to audience.

(41) After position change, all freeze for two to three seconds, Sinky with head in hands, Rocky as 'hero' figure, Chorus as his followers.

One Bod

An introduction

CHARACTERS

Jamie Ruth Hannah Claire PB

THEME 1 Corinthians 12:12-30

Unity. When working in a community better results and greater happiness are achieved by working together, and forgiving each other is vital, as is unselfishness! The sketch benefits from a Bible study and discussion prior to any attempt at staging.

APPROACH

- This sketch relies on the believability of the characters which are very much from real life. It must be performed with pace and energy. Body language, tone of voice and facial expression are vital ingredients of its success. Reaction of one character to another is integral to the sketch, There should be no 'sleeping' partners.
- A workshop based on improvisation techniques would be extremely useful. (See *Rock Solid,* pages 48 and 49, 'Body Shapes', 'Handshake Hullaballoo'. A session on 'Essence Machines', using themes such as 'Division', 'Harmony', 'One World', 'Conflict', would be a useful lead-in to understanding the concept of 'One Body'. See *Rock Solid,* pages 32 and 33.)
- Trust exercises would be beneficial in helping the group to show 'discord' by working as an ensemble. (See *Rock Solid*, page 18, 'Trust', and page 32, 'Blind trust'.)

Catch that cue *(For concentration, eye contact, pace, and picking up on cues!)* (15–20 min)

- Standing in a circle, the leader gives the group a category such as food, TV programmes, parables, football teams, etc. Each person calls out the name of one item from the category as they throw the ball to someone else, e.g. eggs, chips, beans. This acts as a cue for the person who is catching. The leader begins and the ball is passed on until everyone has caught and thrown the ball. The ball must be thrown in sequence every time. No one is allowed to catch the ball twice in one sequence. Whenever there is a mistake, the ball goes back to the leader! Repeat until a rhythm is established and everyone recognises their 'cue'.

  Then the leader takes another *different* coloured ball and chooses a *different* category. In this instance it could be phrases or words from the theme of *One Bod*. The ball must be thrown to a *different* person.

  Then both category balls go round at the same time. When you get proficient you can add a third and a fourth category. Never throw the ball to someone who already has a ball, wait to throw and make sure you have eye contact. Listen for *cues. But this takes time.*

  Project voices, as others won't hear their cue unless you do. All this is like being in a sketch, you have to listen and respond to others at the right time, being sensitive to their needs.

  Some people (there's always one isn't there?) will throw the ball deliberately hard so that it is dropped; emphasise that this is a kind game and that the aim is to work as a team and enable everyone to play their part.

Build each other up, help those who need it. Encourage each other. Think of the theme!

One Bod

SCENE ONE

Sound	*Fucik: 'Entry of the Gladiators', or 'Monty Python' Theme music or similar.*
	(All enter pushing and jostling for position, stand in line in order of speaking) (**1**)
Ruth	*(SR. Positive and cheerful)* All. (**2**)
Jamie	*(On the left of Ruth. Slightly bored)* Are. (**3**)
Hannah	*(CS to the left of Jamie. Nervously)* One. (**4**)
PB	*(CSL to the right of Hannah. Puzzled)* We? (**5**)
Claire	*(SL. Sighing exasperated)* Body! (**6**)
Ruth	*(Sulkily to Jamie)* That's not right, Jamie. It's your fault. *(Bossily sarcastic)* You're in the wrong place. (**7**)
Jamie	*(Very annoyed and showing obvious dislike of being ordered about)* No I'm not. I'm never in the wrong place!
Ruth	Yes you are. *(Moves DSR. Wearily patient)* As per usual.
Jamie	*(Angrily to Ruth)* Oh shut up! I'm sick of you! I don't want to be in it anyway.
	(He exits DSL in a temper) (**8**)
PB	*(Smugly)* Oh well . . . we can't do it then, can we? *(Exits, following Jamie)*
Ruth	Typical! *(Exits DSR)*
Claire and Hannah	*(Look at each other, shrug shoulders and exit together)*

Director's Tips

Starting positions

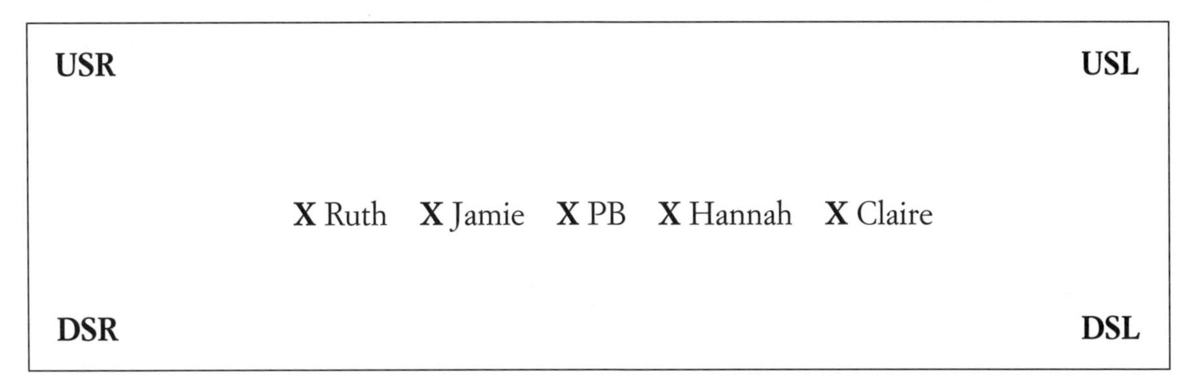

(1) It is important that the entrance appears noisy and chaotic with much pushing, jostling and arguing as they go to position. It must be apparent that Ruth and Jamie are only just tolerating each other.

(2) Ruth must be enthusiastic to the point of irritation. She is a dominant character who always seems to know best!

(3) Jamie thinks he is cool, and that these activities are really beneath him. He is intolerant of girls in general. This must be established from the outset.

(4) Hannah is very polite, and a little nervous in character.

(5) PB is the smallest and the youngest, and does not always concentrate on what he is doing. He'd rather be playing football!

(6) Claire is practical, intelligent and matter-of-fact in her approach. Often the peacemaker.

(7) During the dialogue between Ruth and Jamie, the others stay in position, but react in character. Hannah is worried, Claire is patient, PB is enjoying the fight. The animosity between the two must seem real.

(8) The exit can be into the audience, down an aisle if you feel it works better for your group. It does give the effect of the audience being a party to what's going on! Try it. See if it works.

SCENE TWO

Sound *As before.*

(All enter and stand in line) (**9**)

Jamie *(Sighing reluctantly)* Are. (**10**)

PB *(Yawning loudly)* We. (**11**)

Ruth *(Positively enthusiastic)* All. (**12**)

Hannah *(Sarcastically)* One. (**13**)

Claire *(Muttering)* Body. (**14**)

Hannah *(Irritated)* Claire . . . speak up. We can't *hear* you.

Claire *(Shouting very loudly)* BODY. (**15**)

Ruth *(To Claire)* If you do it like that, you won't get the message through anyway. (**16**)

Claire Well I'm *not* doing it then! *(She exits in a huff)*

Hannah *(To Ruth, accusingly)* Now look what you've done. *(Shouting)* Claire . . . come back! *(She exits after Claire)*

Ruth *(Defensively)* I didn't mean to offend her! *(Exits)* (**17**)

PB I give up! (**18**)

Jamie Let's go and play football. *(They exit together)*

SCENE THREE

Sound *As before.*

(Claire and Ruth enter together. PB and Jamie enter together. Hannah enters alone. Claire ignores her) (**19**)

Hannah *(Pretending not to care)* One.

(9) In silence, avoiding each other. Much glaring between Ruth and Jamie.

USR		**USL**
	X PB **X** Jamie **X** Hannah **X** Claire **X** Ruth	
DSR		**DSL**

(10) Exaggerated boredom, eyes raised, definitely not wanting to be there at all.

(11) Looking at Jamie and following his lead, by yawning loudly and tapping mouth with hand as he does so, tapping foot and trying to be 'cool'.

(12) Desperately trying to counteract the oppressive atmosphere, she is over the top in her enthusiasm, and disappointed when it appears to have no effect.

(13) Hannah has really given up any idea that they can achieve anything, and is extremely sarcastic in tone.

(14) Claire's reaction as she listens to the others is the realisation that things are not going to work out. Nobody hears her muttered comment, including the audience.

(15) It is really important that this is shouted in an extremely loud and angry voice, as she stares ahead in anger.

(16) Ruth must be patronising in the extreme when she delivers this comment, the last straw that breaks the camel's back!

(17) Ruth is quite genuinely puzzled that she has upset Claire. She doesn't realise how patronising she sounds! She weeps as she exits.

(18) The two boys have listened to this exchange with superior attitude. PB is relieved to have any excuse to give up, and this must be clear in his voice, facial expression and body language. Jamie too would rather play football than sort out relationship problems with 'women'! They could have a mock football game as they exit. (In mime of course.)

(19) They need to take a long way round to get to their places, showing definite divisions, and ignoring each other. Sly whispers about each other can be improvised. Ruth, however, has obviously made it up with Claire, but Hannah must be seen to be 'missed out' and uncomfortable. Body language, facial expression are vital here as all the nuances of grudges, dislikes and failed relationships must be communicated to the audience in this short entrance. Experiment with different ideas, before fixing on the one that works best.

USR		**USL**
	X Hannah **X** Jamie **X** PB **X** Ruth **X** Claire	
DSR		**DSL**

Jamie	Are Are Are Are Are Are ARE! (**20**)
Ruth	*(Disgusted with Jamie)* All. (**21**)
Claire	*(Glaring at Jamie)* Body.
PB	*(Sighing)* We.
Ruth	That's wrong. (**22**)
	(All argue loudly, picking fault with each other. PB covers his ears) (**23**)
PB	*(Shouting)* STOP! *(All suddenly stop and look at him in amazement)* *(Resignedly patient)* I'll tell you what. I'm the smallest so I'll go at the front. *(He moves to the beginning of the line, the rest shuffle back to their places)* *(Loudly enthusiastic)* WE. (**24**)
Hannah	*(Hopefully)* One?
Jamie	*(Resigned)* Are!
Ruth	*(Hopefully)* All?
Claire	*(Satisfied for a moment that it is right)* Body. (**25**)
All	*(Realise it's wrong again and look at each other desperately)*
Jamie	*(Deliberately unkind)* I'm not standing next to Ruth. She smells! (**26**)
Ruth	Don't flatter yourself. I don't want you to stand next to *me* either. *(She bursts into tears)* I've had enough of you, *you . . .* *(She exits crying)* (**27**)
Hannah	That was *so* mean! *(Runs off after Ruth)* (**27**)
Jamie	*(Mimicking Hannah)* That was *so* mean!

(20) Deliberately mocking tone, head moving in rhythm from side to side as words are spoken very childishly. The others glance at him with various reactions, only PB finds it funny.

(21) Ruth must show all her dislike of Jamie in her tone of voice and expression as she speaks.

(22) Very concerned, but misinterpreted by all the others as yet more criticism!

(23) This is an improvised argument, which must be very loud and aggressive. Each person must argue with at least two others, almost coming to blows, in order to upset PB and make him want to stop it. Don't let it last longer than a minute or the audience will be bored, if you can get the same effect in less time then you're brill!

(24) PB is trying to give the impression that he is being very 'adult'. His 'We' must inspire the others to really try harder.

(25) It is important that the realisation that it is still wrong 'dawns' over Claire's face and that abject depression is shown in her expression after she has spoken. At the same time, the others look at each other desperately, one should get the feeling that they were confident that it might be right and are now extremely frustrated.

(26) Jamie realises that he is standing next to Ruth and takes out his frustration on her by being incredibly unkind and personal. Really emphasise the lines, sufficiently to alienate the audience, who must really dislike Jamie at this point.

(27) The next lines up to the exit must have pace (jumping in on cues) and be spoken with energy. The audience must almost heave a sigh of relief that the torment is not to go on any longer. They too should feel the frustration.

Claire We're never going to get it together. Ever! *(She exits)*

PB Never! *(He exits)*

Jamie *(Pulling a face)* I don't care! *(Exits)*

SCENE FOUR

Sound *As before.*

(Jamie and Ruth sulkily move away from each other as they enter, miserably, the others slowly slink into position. Ruth stands apart from the rest DSL) (**28**)

PB *(CSL. To Ruth)* We *need* you, Ruth. (**29**)

Jamie *(Moving DSR)* We *don't* need her. (**30**)

Claire *(CSR. Moves to Jamie DSR)* But who's *we*? (**31**)

Jamie *(Mocking)* We? Us! *All* of us!

Claire *(Irritated with him)* We *need* ALL then, don't we? *(Moves to Ruth)* Of course we need you. (**32**)

Jamie *(Unkindly)* No we don't. (**33**)

Ruth *(Sulkily)* I'm not doing it until *he* apologises.

Jamie *(Moving USRC with back to Ruth) I'm* not apologising.

PB *(Persuasively to Ruth)* We?

Jamie *(Turning sulkily)* Are!

Hannah *(CS. Positively)* One. (**34**)

(Hannah, Jamie and PB realise that they have made sense and are excited. Jamie moves to Hannah CS) (**35**)

PB *(Running to R of Jamie)* We.

Jamie *(Enthusiastically)* Are.

(**28**) It is a good idea for Ruth and Jamie to enter first, meet in the middle and deliberately avoid each other as they go to their positions.

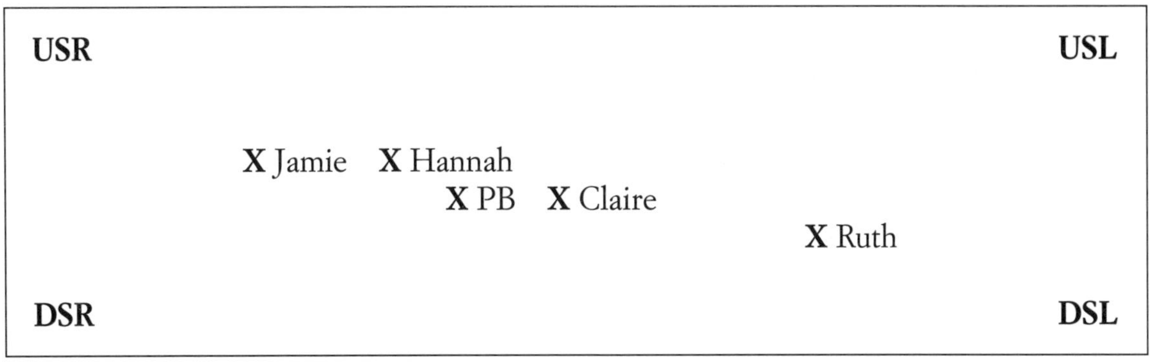

USR				**USL**
	X Jamie	**X** Hannah		
		X PB **X** Claire		
			X Ruth	
DSR				**DSL**

(**29**) PB must show here that he has had a change of heart and is sincerely trying to be kind as he speaks to Ruth.

(**30**) Aggressively sulky.

(**31**) Genuinely trying to solve the problem as she moves to Jamie.

(**32**) Trying to placate Ruth, by being sympathetic. Ruth is secretly pleased that she is wanted after all, and turns as if to join them.

(**33**) Ruth reacts by returning to her place DSR, annoyed.

(**34**) Hannah tries hard to be positive and enthusiastic here.

(**35**) The enthusiasm that follows when they make sense at last must be really infectious. Much bounce and positive body language. They are extremely self-congratulatory.

Hannah *(Shouting triumphantly)* One.

Hannah, Jamie, PB We are one. *(Chanting and jumping around in triumph)*

Jamie *(Bursting into laughter and pointing at Ruth)* We don't need you! (**36**)

Claire, Ruth *(Look at each other in desperation, link arms and retaliate loudly)* ALL BODY! ALL BODY! (**37**)

(The two groups become chaotic and aggressive, repeating their phrases over and over again. All bump, Ruth falls DSC and is really hurt. Jamie reluctantly helps her up) (**38**)

Jamie *(Sincerely concerned)* Are you OK? Sorry!

Ruth Yes. I'll live. *(Pause)* I'm sorry too.

(All move into line, Jamie helps Ruth, Claire and Hannah hug, PB beams at everyone. Hesitantly they begin again, willing it to be right, and supporting each other)

PB *(DSR)* We. (**39**)

Jamie *(To right of PB)* Are.

Ruth *(CS. Slightly excited)* All.

Hannah *(To right of Ruth. Excited)* One.

Claire *(DSL. Thrilled)* Body.

PB *(Jubilant)* We are all one body!

All *(Chanting happily, weaving in and out. Slapping hands, dancing with glee as they repeat . . .)* We are all one body! We are all one body! We are all one body! We are all one body!

(They exit exuberantly, repeating the words as they go and also moving in unison) (**40**)

Sound *As before.*

(**36**) Jamie must be annoyingly triumphant, gloating over the other two. Their disappointed and angry reaction points the division further.

(**37**) Ruth and Claire can-can step as they repeat their words.

(**38**) It is effective if the two groups challenge each other like two gangs as they repeat their words, getting closer and closer until Ruth falls. It is important that Jamie is the one to cause the accident. His reaction on seeing the hurt he has caused must be genuine, and so must Ruth's response. It is important that the other three react with relief that the rift appears to be healed.

(**39**) It is important here that as the sentence begins to make sense, the excitement grows, building to a climax as PB shouts 'We are all one body' in triumph.

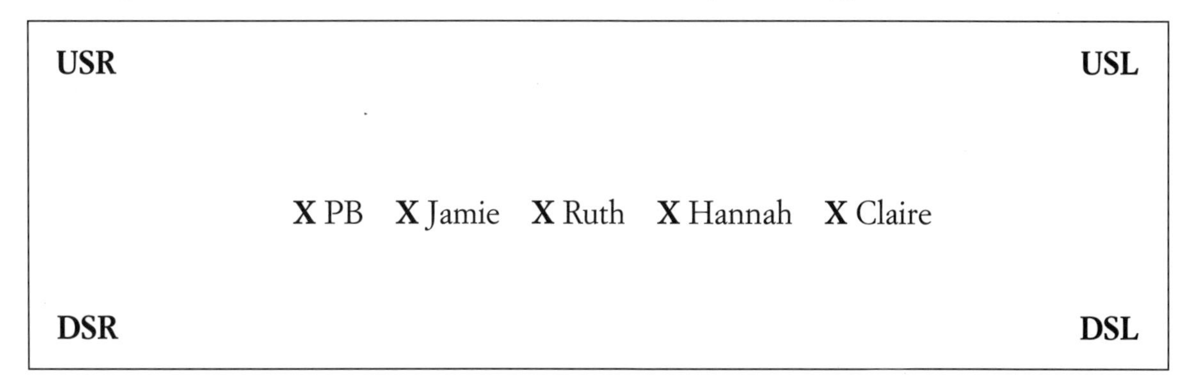

(**40**) It is as well if the group work out their own moves with the director, as it will depend very much on the space in which the sketch is being presented. It is effective if they can move through or around the audience. It is also possible to get the audience to join hands and chant along with them, but don't force this, judge your audience mood carefully!

Once Upon a Time
An introduction

CHARACTERS

Narrators 1 and 2	*Mr Creep*	*Mrs Pride*	*Ms Prayloud*
Mr Showoff	*Ms Lookatme*	*Mr Needy*	

THEME Matthew 6:1-24

Don't be a hypocrite. Don't proclaim your good deeds to the world. Be sensitive to those around you.

APPROACH

This is a fun sketch in the fairy story/children's tale genre with a serious message for all ages. It must be played with pace and attack. Much depends on the physical changes from neutral to character which must be maintained all the way through. The moves are original but feel free to develop them as appropriate for your group. A workshop on characterisation would be very useful prior to the sketch being staged (see *Develop Your Skills,* also *Rock Solid* – 'Characterisation'). Freeze frame is important to focus on the relevant action. (See *Quick Pics* in *Develop Your Skills.*)

Changing character

Musical hats

Equipment: at least one hat for each member of the group, lots of variety. Cassette player.

- All stand in a circle. Each person is given a hat. The music plays and when it stops all take on a character suitable to the hat they are wearing and speak and act according to that character, moving around the space.
- The leader can freeze the action at any time and point to one person who continues to improvise. A tambour drum is useful here. Encourage them to think about posture, type of voice, accent, etc.
- *Individual improvisation:* All hats are placed in the centre of the circle, a ball is passed from one to another; when the music stops, whoever holds the ball rushes to the centre, picks up a hat and improvises in character. He/she continues to wear the hat until everyone has had a turn. Get them to really exaggerate the voice and movement of the characters in preparation for the sketch.
- *Group improvisation:* All split into twos or threes, the ball is thrown from one group to another at random. When the music stops, the group holding the ball, using the idea of the hat character, devise a short, spontaneous piece. When the music begins, play resumes as usual.

  Development: Give them time to develop one of the ideas, about 10 minutes, and let them perform for the group. Then get them to perform the same piece only much larger than life, to a ridiculous degree. When everyone has picked themselves up off the floor and the laughter has subsided, introduce the 'Once Upon a Time' sketch.

Once Upon a Time

(All characters are standing upstage with backs to the audience in neutral, except the narrators who are situated DSR and DSL and Mr Needy who sits in a cardboard box CSR looking very sad and hungry) (**1**)

Narrator 1 *(DSR)* Once upon a time in a magic land. (**2**)

Narrator 2 *(DSL)* Where the sky was always blue.

All *(Turning briefly to look over left shoulders)* Blue! (**3**)

Narrator 2 And the sun was always shining.

All *(Turning briefly to look over right shoulders)* Sunshine! (**4**)

Narrator 1 There lived Mr Needy. (**5**)

Mr Needy I haven't any **cash!** (**6**)
I haven't got a **home**
I haven't got a **single thing**
To **call my own**.

Narrator 1 Poor Mr Needy. He lived in a cardboard box on the High Street. He hoped and he hoped that someone would help him. (**7**)

Narrator 2 Then . . . along came Mr Showoff.

Mr Showoff *(Turns and moves diagonally DSC, stylised movement. Singing or speaking in rhythm)* (**8**)

I can dance,
I can talk,
the hunky thing about me
is the way that I walk. (**9**)

Director's Tips

Starting positions

USR					**USL**
			Mrs Lookatme		
	Mr Creep **X**	**X**	**X**	**X**	**X**
		Mrs Pride		Ms Prayloud	Mr Showoff
		X Mr Needy			
X Narrator 1					Narrator 2 **X**
DSR					**DSL**

(1) At this point no one, except Mr Needy, is in character. The Narrators stand relaxed making eye contact with the audience. Mr Needy huddles on or in his cardboard box. The others stand in 'neutral' upstage.

(2) The Narrators have the responsibility of telling the story with exaggerated emphasis as if to a small child. Think of the whole thing as a kind of cartoon! Lay extra stress on important words in sentences, and be prepared to slow down the narration in parts. The narrator is in collusion with the audience in that he/she knows that they know that he/she knows that it is over the top! (If you see what I mean?)

3)(4) The characters upstage assist the narrator at this point, and echoing the story-telling tone of voice, turn, in unison, in the same direction, gain eye contact with the audience, and say 'blue'. Immediately turn back into neutral. This is a recurring element in the sketch and needs to be 'spot on' if it is to have the most impact, so spend time on getting it right!

5) Gesturing towards Mr Needy, then listening with interest to what he has to say, perhaps a sad shake of the head here?

6) Mr Needy might hold out a hat as if asking for money as he speaks in rhythm, really milking it for sympathy. The character needs to be a stereotypical Mr Man.

7) The Narrator's voice and expression should echo in a slightly melodramatic way, Mr Needy's plight.

8) All the characters need to take note of this. As each character is brought into the action they go through a series of movements as follows: turn quickly to face audience in neutral; assume statue of their character, hold for a second; move as their character and become part of the scene. This establishes the stylised form the story takes. Mr Showoff is an expansive character, and could have a large cheque book, or a top hat, or some other prop symbolising great wealth. Maybe a large pound sign would do it? Just choose one, too many props can distract from the action.

) As with all the other characters, Mr Showoff needs a specific way of walking, and a voice which reflects his self-importance and pomposity and greed. Some work on characterisation stereotypes would help all the characters to work towards this, before even attempting the sketch. (See *Rock Solid,* page 34, 'Characterisation Stereotypes'. Create your own Mr Men character cards!) The words must be spoken in rhythm (They can be sung in a parody of the well-known Phil Collins song!) The rhythm goes as follows – lines 1 and 2 on three sharp beats, lines 3 and 4 fitted between two slow beats. This applies to all repeats of this motif by other characters. Staccato delivery helps to continue the illusion of fairy story.

1	2	3	1	2	3	1 2	1 2
I	**can**	**dance**	**I**	**can**	**talk**	The **hun**ky thing a**bout** me	Is the **way** that I **walk**

Others	*(Turn and thumb noses at him)* Mr Showoff! *(Turn back)* (**10**)
Narrator 1	This fella is hunky . . . (**11**)
Mr Showoff	*(Hunky pose)* (**12**)
Narrator 2	Handsome.
Mr Showoff	*(Handsome pose)*
Narrator 2	He spends his days.
Mr Showoff	*(Interrupting boastfully)* Six days a week.
Narrator 1	Working hard as an entrepreneur . . . (**13**)
Others	*(Turn to narrator with a sarcastic yet dumb expression)* A what?
Mr Showoff	*(Interrupting boastfully)* Entrepreneur . . . in the best part of town of course! (**14**)
Others	*(Turn back in unison)*
Narrator 1	Of course!
Mr Showoff	*(Move SL to Narrator 2 smugly)* I work very, very hard. I earn lots and lots and lots of money! *(Gleefully shouting across to Narrator 1)* And I like to spend it too!
Narrator 2	*(Suspiciously)* Lots of money? (**15**)
Others	*(Turn to face audience)* Pots and pots of it! *(Turn back)* (**16**)
Mr Showoff	*(Defensively)* But I give a lot away! Mr Creep handles that!
	(Mr Creep turns, assumes humble stance and walks from USR to left of Mr Showoff) (**17**)
Narrator 1	This is Mr Creep.

(10) See (**3**). Remember identical, sharp and controlled movement is more effective than sloppy stuff.

(11) Spoken as if on a TV advert for the latest pop idol, film star, or jeans!

(12) Almost simultaneously take up muscle man pose and freeze for a second until the Narrator's next speech suggests a change of pose. Change on 'handsome' to a 'male model' (in an expensive Italian suit) pose!

(13) Show high pleasure at the use of a long word, the meaning of which is probably unknown!

(14) The first part of this is split into syllables and spoken as if to a very dozy child. If Narrator 2 joins in with the 'A what?' then Mr Showoff can address 'ent-re-pre-neur' in that direction.

(15) The implication being that Mr Showoff is selfish and that he ought to share it a bit. Mr Showoff doesn't want people to dislike him and must jump in on his next line quickly. Excuses! Excuses!

(16) Turn with right shoulder, sideways with face to audience, bringing up right arm in expansive gesture. As soon as line is delivered bring arm back as if bowling overarm and let the momentum turn you with backs to audience. If you can't cope with that make up your own gesture, but make it big, and act 'as one'.

(17) Turn on 'Mr Creep'.

Mr Creep I can sing, (**18**)
I can walk,
the creepy thing about me
is the way that I talk.

Narrator 2 *(Imitating him)* He can sing.

Narrator 1 *(Imitating him)* He can walk.

Others *(Turning)* The creepy thing about him is the way that he talks. (**19**)

Mr Creep I can sell anything to anyone; better than Saatchi and Saatchi. Mr Showoff is my best client. He pays well too!

Mr Showoff Mr Creep gives my money to *big* charities. And he advertises my amazing generosity all over the place, so that everyone will know in Mr Men Land . . . just what a wonderfully kind person I am. Mr Generous – that's me. (**20**)

Narrator 1 Mr Showoff lives in a lovely house.

Narrator 2 With a lovely garden.

Narrator 1 In Opulent Avenue.

Mr Showoff I have *lovely* neighbours.

Narrators Miss Lookatme! (**21**)

Ms Lookatme *(Turns USC moves CS)*
Look at me, (**22**)
I'm the best.
The smashin' thing about me is
I'm better than the rest.

Oh Mr Needy Person. Watch, everybody! I'm going to give some sympathy to this *needy person!* There you go, Mr Needy . . . *lots* of sympathy from *me. (She pats Mr Needy on the head)* Poor Mr Needy. *(To the audience)* Did you see what I did? Did you? I am *so* kind. Did you see? Are you watching? Are you? (**23**)

(**18**) See (**8**) and (**9**).

(**19**) As they turn, imitate *briefly* Mr Creep's slimy movement, and then turn back.

(**20**) This must be really expansive and addressed to the audience. He agrees smugly to the Narrator's description of his living conditions.

(**21**) As if introducing a circus act, with a gesture towards her. Mr Creep and Mr Showoff also focus their gaze on her.

(**22**) See (**8**) and (**9**).

(**23**) This must be really exaggerated and insincere, with much emphasis on drawing attention to herself.

All We're watching.

Narrator 1 Along came Mrs Pride.

Mrs Pride *(Turns, moves CS)* (**24**)

Narrator 2 She didn't even notice Miss Lookatme!

Mrs Pride I'm so great, (**25**)
I'm so good.
I always do the Christian thing
the way that I should!

Narrator 1 She's so great.

Narrator 2 She's so good.

Mr Showoff She always does the Christian thing. *(Move USR with back to audience)* (**26**)

Mr Creep The way that she should! *(Move USR with back to audience and to right of Mr Showoff)* (**27**)

Ms Lookatme Huh! *(Move USL with back to audience and to right of Ms Prayloud)*

Mrs Pride *(Using Mr Needy's box as a lectern)* Good afternoon everyone. I'd like to tell you about myself. I go to church, every Sunday, morning and evening. I always have done, ever since I was a child. I've hardly missed a day. My mother ran the Sunday school and of course I intend to follow in her footsteps. (**28**)

Narrator 1 Mrs Pride has all kinds of church duties at Mr Men Church including organising the Fund for the Elderly.

Mrs Pride *(Moving CS)* Don't forget that I'm also Chairperson of the Mrs Fellowship! (**29**)

Narrator 2 She attends choir practice every Wednesday.

(24) See (**8**) and (**9**). Mrs Pride comes forward between Ms Lookatme and Mr Needy, arrogantly pushing her out of the way. Ms Lookatme reacts with irritation and moves US glaring at Mrs Pride.

(25) See (**9**).

(26) Turn with back to audience in neutral.

(27) Turn with back to audience in neutral.

(28) Moves to address this to Mr Needy.

(29) Addresses this confidentially to the audience.

Mrs Pride *And* I help out with the church tea rota. Don't forget my work in the Oxfam shop, the arranging of flowers for the services, I read the lesson every week and . . . (**30**)

Narrator 1 She lives on Organisation Street.

Mrs Pride I am an absolute genius at organisation. Why, you just give . . .

All *(Turn)* Thank you, Mrs Pride. (**31**)

Mrs Pride *(To Mr Needy)* Must go anyway. Haven't time for idle chatter. I have to polish the altar rail. I take great pride in that you know. *(Confidentially to Narrator 1 DSR)* I'm having afternoon tea with Mr Spoutalot. He's the vicar, you know.

All *(Turn and look over left shoulders)* We know! *(Turn back)* (**32**)

Mrs Pride *(She moves USR and Across to stand to left of Ms Lookatme)*

Narrator 2 Along came Miss Prayloud. (**33**)

Miss Prayloud *(Turns and moves CS)* (**34**)

Narrator 1 She didn't notice Mr Needy either.

Miss Prayloud I can sing (**35**)
I can pray
I pray loud on street corners and
I do it every day!

Others *(Turning briefly)* She does it *every* day! (**36**)

Miss Prayloud Roll up. Roll up, everyone. Are you listening? There's nothing like a good pray to keep the wolf from the door! Hallelujah. Praise the Lord! Listen . . . can you hear? I raise my voice as loud as I can so folk can hear, real clear. *(singing)* (**37**)

Oh God, our help in ages past,
oh God, you are so good
to let me pray so publicly
just the way I should.

(30) As if ticking off a list. She could take a diary out of her handbag and leaf through it as she speaks.

(31) Fingers under noses in 'snob' gesture, and freeze until next speech.

(32) Spoken in unison, with the tone of voice implying that they've heard it all before. Turn back immediately after speaking.

(33) Narrators put hands together on 'Prayloud'.

(34) See (**8**).

(35) See (**9**).

(36) As she speaks her voice gets louder and louder and all put their hands over their ears, before turning back.

(37) She sings in a mock operatic voice, but making sure that her diction is clear and that the sound grates on the ears. The others keep their hands over their ears although still with backs to the audience. Each back tells a story of sheer horror at the sound.

I do this, Lord, so all will know
that I'm a friend of yours,
I pray out loud wherever I can,
I very rarely pause.

(Spoken) Hallelujah! *(to Mr Needy as she moves back to USC in line)* You should try it sometime. It'll do you a power of good! (**38**)

All *(Move forward repeating their rhymes and freeze)*

Narrator 1 Make sure you do not perform your religious duties in public,

(Mrs Pride changes pose) (**39**)

so that people will see what you do. If you do these things publicly, you will not have any reward from your Father in Heaven.

(Ms Lookatme changes pose) (**40**)

Narrator 2 And when you give something to a needy person, do not make a big show of it as the hypocrites do in the houses of worship and on the streets. *(Mr Showoff and Mr Creep change poses)* (**41**)

Narrator 1 They do it so that people will praise them. I assure you they've already been paid in full. *(Ms Prayloud changes pose)* (**42**)

Narrator 2 When you pray, do it in such a way that even your closest friend will not know about it.

All *(Turn with backs to audience in neutral)* (**43**)

Narrator 2 Then it will be a private matter.

(Moves to Mr Needy and secretly gives him a large sandwich and stands SL with back to audience) (**44**)

Mr Needy *(Says grace in mime before he eats with relish)* (**45**)

(**38**) Mr Needy stares straight ahead in abject misery. Other characters turn on 'power' in character.

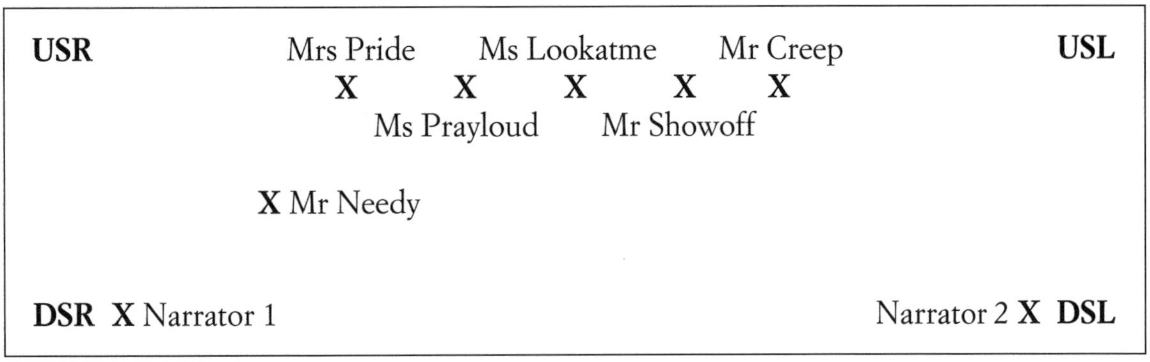

USR	Mrs Pride	Ms Lookatme	Mr Creep	**USL**
	X **X**	**X**	**X** **X**	
	Ms Prayloud		Mr Showoff	
	X Mr Needy			
DSR **X** Narrator 1				Narrator 2 **X** **DSL**

(**39**) Assuming a prayer or singing position, very expansive.

(**40**) Pointing to herself and looking smug.

(**41**) Using aspects of their characters which are typical, but working together.

(**42**) Kneeling in prayer, but with eyes open to check that she is being watched.

(**43**) This must not be sloppy but efficient and quick. Make sure that all are upstage of Mr Needy. As they turn, Narrator 2 speaks and then moves to mask Mr Needy and then joins the upstage line in neutral.

(**44**) All are very still as the need is to focus on Mr Needy as he gazes hungrily at the food.

(**45**) He collects himself halfway to taking the first bite, puts down the sandwich, looks up to heaven gratefully with hands in prayer and then eats hungrily.

Narrator 1 *(Looking at Mr Needy)* And your Father, who sees what you do in private will reward you. (**46**)

(ALL FREEZE) (**47**)

(46) Narrator 1 looks at Mr Needy and does not speak to the audience until he begins to eat.

(47) Narrator 1 turns back to audience as all freeze. Hold the freeze for 3-5 seconds.

Paradise Lost

An introduction

CHARACTERS

Pilot   *Hostess*   *Mrs Binge*   *Mr Binge*   *Miss Binge*

THEME Matthew 19:16-19; Mark 10:17-30; Luke 18:18-30
The sketch is based on the parable of the rich young ruler.

APPROACH

This sketch is almost a series of changing tableaux or Quick Pics with dialogue. It depends very much on the freeze frames to communicate the feelings of the Binge family. A breakdown of these freeze frames in a Quick Pic exercise would help in the development of the characters. This sketch must go at quite a pace in order to be effective.

Stretch that imagination!

Machines (A moving Quick Pic!)

- In groups of four or five create the following machines or objects, and on a given signal move them appropriately. All work at the same time. E.g. *lawnmower, toaster, foodmixer, typewriter, cassette player, washing machine, etc.*
- Allow only a limited time to make each machine (2 minutes at the most). Let the groups demonstrate. Encourage them to add sounds. Remind them about plugs and switches, etc.
- Bring them to life on a signal *(drum beat).* Freeze them again.
- Stress the need for safety when several people are working together like this. It must be very carefully worked out, unless you like having a foot in your mouth, or someone sitting on your head!

Group improvisation

Who, where, what, when, why

Divide into groups of three (up to five if necessary, but three is best).

Prepare five sets of cards and give them out as follows:
WHO – containing a character outline *one for every person* in the group. E.g. *Policeman, alien.*
WHERE – containing a location – *one per group.* E.g. *In a supermarket, in a sports hall, in heaven.*
WHAT – containing a suggested prop – *one per group.* E.g. *A bouquet of roses, smelly socks.*
WHEN – containing the time of the incident – *one per group. Late at night, 4 am.*
WHY – Contains a possible situation – *one per group. After a storm, middle of a family row.*

They devise a short piece either spontaneously or within a given time limit. (No longer than 20 minutes).

Some really strange combinations arise, and it really stretches the imagination to link them together, remain in character, and make sense out of apparent nonsense!

Share each scene when they are complete, and remember to encourage positive criticism and discourage negative remarks by looking at ways to improve and develop the ideas.

Paradise Lost

(Frozen tableau, with Pilot DSL, Hostess DSR, Mr and Mrs Binge CS linking arms, Miss Binge kneeling in front of them sucking her thumb) (**1**)

Pilot *(To audience)* Good evening, ladies and gentlemen. Thank you for flying Paradise Travel! (**2**)

Hostess *(To audience)* We'd like you to give a special welcome to the Binge family from Bolton. (**3**)

Pilot *(To audience)* Let's hear it for the Binge family!

All Hooray! *(All cheer, clap, stamp, etc.)* (**4**)

Hostess *(Addressing the audience)* They are en route to their *final destination.*

Pilot The kingdom . . . (**5**)

Hostess Of heaven. (**5**)

Pilot *(Addressing the audience)* So – put your hands together for the kingdom of heaven!

All Hooray! *(Cheer, clap, stamp, etc.)* (**4**)

Mrs Binge *(To Mr B, concerned)* Oh dear, I hope we've packed everything, darling. The digital TV, the microwave, the mobile phone, the PC. Did I bring the dishwasher?

Mr Binge *(Patronising)* I *think* we've packed everything. *(To hostess)* We'll be there soon, eh? Safe journey?

Pilot Fasten your seat belts.

Binges Zzzzzzzzzzzzzip! Clunk! *(All mime action then immediately light cigarettes)* (**6**)

Hostess *(With disapproving look)* And extinguish your cigarettes. (**7**)

Director's Tips

Starting positions

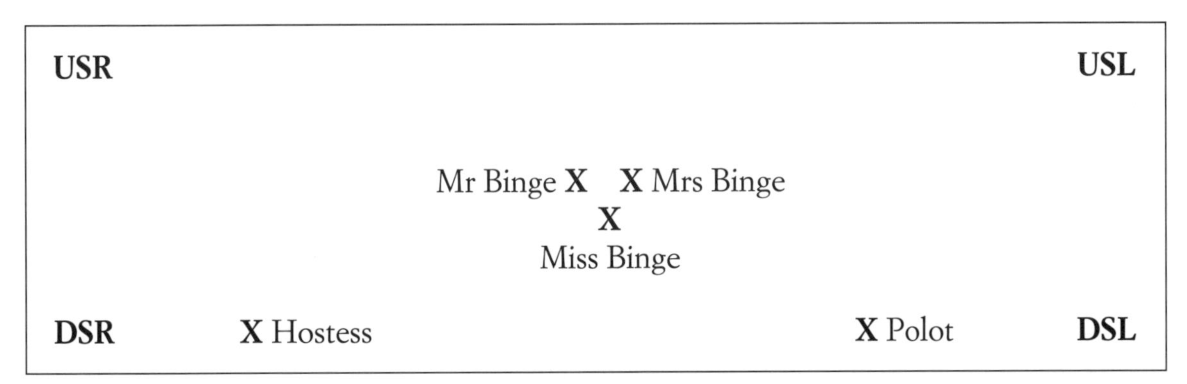

(1) It is vital that the initial tableau is totally still, in order to focus on the Binge family and tell the audience about them, i.e. they are self-satisfied, and the daughter is young and spoilt.

2) The pilot should be full of energy, and lines should be delivered in the style of an advert, or an enthusiastic game show host. Addressing the audience direct, and involving them is very important.

3) This character, as also the Pilot, must deliver lines with the forced jollity of a tour rep! Eye contact with the audience is a 'must'.

4) Pilot and Hostess clapping enthusiastically, encouraging the audience to do likewise. The Binges, all together, come out of their 'freeze'. Mr and Mrs clap in an embarrassed way, but Miss Binge is violently enthusiastic and has to be restrained by her parents. This 'in and out' of freeze helps to establish the 'cartoon', stylised nature of the sketch from the beginning. They immediately freeze again as before.

5) 'Kingdom' and 'Heaven' must be delivered as a game show host warming up the audience.

6) On 'zzzip' pull seat belt up and across with left hand, and fasten on 'Click'. Accuracy, and moving exactly together emphasises the comic element of the sketch. It will take practice to get moves at exactly the same angle and identical.

7) A glance at the Binges as they light cigarettes, which must be done at speed, prior to speaking. The Binges react in an embarrassed way, firstly trying to hide their cigarettes, and then hurriedly looking for somewhere to extinguish them.

Mr and Mrs	Sssssssssssss. *(Put cigarettes out on daughter's head)* (**8**)
Miss Binge	*(Glaring up at them)* Ow!
Pilot	Say your prayers.
Mr Binge	*(Offended, defensive)* We always do! *(Binges into prayer positions)* (**9**)
Pilot	And hope for a safe landing. *(Binges open their eyes and look up in horror)* (**10**)
Miss Binge	*(Very loudly)* Amen! *(All Binges snore in tableau)* (**11**) *and* (**12**)
Mrs Binge	*(In her sleep)* Have I done the washing-up?
Binges	*(Suddenly awake)* Later on . . . (**13**)
Pilot	Here we are! (**14**)
Hostess	At the airport of Paradise.
Binges	*(Excited tableau)* Ah! (**15**)
Pilot	Time is running out. (**16**)
Binges	*(Worried tableau)* Oh! (**17**)
Hostess	*(Very cheerfully as if to reassure)* But the weather is fine.
Binges	Aaaaaah! *(Sigh in anticipation. Blissful thoughts tableau)* (**17**)
Pilot	We hope you've enjoyed your trip.
Binges	*(Politely. Polite tableau)* Mmmmmmmm! (**17**)
Hostess	Have a nice day. *(Hostess and pilot kneel CS, face front, form gates)* (**18**)
Binges	*(Leaning forward smugly)* We always do!

(8) Actions must be exactly together. The daughter's reaction exaggerated, but instant. The whole of the sketch must have pace and energy.

(9) It is effective if Mrs glares at Hostess and Mr at Pilot, while Miss looks up at parents, apparently copying their attitude. Immediate Quick Pic of exaggerated piety. NB: Remember, stylised and 'over the top' at all times, plus precision and accuracy of mime.

(10) Quick change of position as Mr and Mrs open their eyes.

(11) As Miss B, obviously frightened, says 'amen', perhaps throwing arms akimbo, parents give her a quick nudge prior to sudden return to 'piety pic' which is held for a very short time.

(12) Slow sagging and leaning on each other as they begin to snore and piety pic melts into sleeping, tossing and turning. Mrs B mumbles as if asleep, but it must be heard by the audience over the snores and whistles of Mr B.

(13) Sudden exaggerated energy, and direct address to the audience.

(14) The next three speeches should be delivered with pace, each comment building to a pitch of excitement from the Binges.

(15) Much exaggerated energy as they move into new tableau, facial expressions vital.

(16) Melodramatically, as a warning. Think again of quiz show host!

(17) The excited, tense anticipation sags, suddenly deflated. Body language is very important here, especially as the Binges gather themselves together to respond in a falsely polite manner to the next comment.

(18) Form gates by joining one hand each. This move must be precise and quick; there is nothing worse than sloppy movement to detract from the focus of a sketch.

Miss Binge	*(Exuberantly)* Look. *(Points excitedly at the 'gates')*
All Binges	It's the *Pearly* gates! *(Wild stylised actions)* (**19**)
Pilot	Customs!
Pilot/Hostess	Anything to declare?
Binges	*(Offended)* No! Of course not! (**20**)
Hostess/Pilot	Luggage over there. *(Gesturing upstage)*
Mr Binge	Everything? (**21**)
Hostess	*(Firmly)* Everything!
Mrs Binge	*(Horrified)* Everything?
Pilot	*(Extremely firm)* Everything!
Binges	*(Crossly)* Everything? *(Wink knowingly at audience and run USC). In unison move US, put down luggage and hide things up jumpers behind backs as they speak, etc.)* (**22**) (**23**)
Mrs Binge	Oh darling . . . we must take the video camera. (**24**)
Mr Binge	*(Thinks)* Oooh . . . I don't know!
Mrs Binge	*(Impatiently)* Oh! I'll put it under my coat! *(She does so)*
Mr Binge	I must take my mobile phone, with superb reception, and immediate replacement on loss. It's good to talk! *(Mimes mobile, slips it down sock)*
Miss Binge	*(Sulkily persistent)* But Muuuum . . . I simply can't *survive* without my computer! (**25**)
Mr and Mrs	*(Exasperated. Look at each other, advance on her)* Down the hatch. (**26**)
Miss Binge	*(Gulps down the computer painfully).* (**27**)

(**19**) Exaggerated enthusiasm in the voice, plus over-exaggerated, wild, stylised actions, rather 'David Bellamy', which finally freeze focused on the 'gate' at exactly the same time.

(**20**) Lean back, all together on 'no' and holding the freeze during the next line points their reaction.

(**21**) Lean forward in unison to emphasise the horror and surprise at having to leave everything. Also the next four speeches must be very fast, on cue, without losing the different tones of voice. Tone of voice and facial expression are vital in this sketch, otherwise the comedy is totally lost. It all depends very much on action and reaction.

(**22**) The family must lean forward to the audience and appear to expect their collaboration in twisting the customs. The wink therefore must be exaggerated with the whole body, and performed in total unison.

(**23**) Turn and move exactly together in conspiratorial fashion.

(**24**) Looking over her shoulder as she speaks to check that she is not being overheard. Mr B mimes using a mobile, getting through on 'It's good to talk', then swiftly pocketing it with a furtive glance to see that he is not being watched.

(**25**) Moving CS. Speaking loudly enables the parents to react in an exasperated way. Again action and reaction.

(**26**) It helps here if one parent holds her head and the other pushes large computer down her throat. Move away immediately, so that the audience can see fully her mime of swallowing it.

(**27**) Over-the-top facial expression here as she swallows, followed by relief, and finally self-satisfaction.

Mr Binge	*(Patting her on the head, and she grins, self-satisfied)* Good girl.
All	Here we go. Through the pearly gates. *(They move DS, gates open briefly, they tentatively, rather guiltily try to step through)* (**28**) *and* (**29**)
Hostess/Pilot	*(Together, loudly)* BEEEEEEP!
Binges	*(Hurriedly step back in a tableau of shock)* (**30**)
Mr Binge	*(Angry and surprised)* Beep?
Hostess	*(Matter of fact)* Beep.
Mrs Binge	*(Incredulously)* Beep?
Pilot	*(Firmly)* Beep.
Miss Binge	*(Shrilly)* BEEEEEEEEEP! (**31**)
Mr and Mrs	*(Hit her)* Shut up, dear! *(She is upset. All look at hostess)* (**32**)
Hostess	Article 777 states that *no* encumbrances shall be brought into the kingdom of heaven. *(All Binges look at pilot)*
Pilot	All possessions shall be *voluntarily* discarded on the way. *Before* entry.
Binges	*(Horrified)* Discarded?
Miss Binge	But that's *awful!* (**33**)
Mr and Mrs	*Awful!* (**33**)
Mr Binge	*(Ingratiatingly to Pilot, plays with pilot's hair absentmindedly)* But, er, we, er, always, er, we always do everything *right*. We *never* do anything wrong. (**34**)
Mrs Binge	*(To Hostess, defensive)* We go to church *every* Sunday you know! We *never* miss!

(28) This line is spoken in 'game show host' style, forced and exaggerated.

(29) This series of actions needs to be carefully rehearsed, so that the breaking of hands coincides exactly with the toes over the line, etc., otherwise the whole thing will look messy, and everyone could end up in an undignified heap on the floor!

(30) A swift tableau here with the dialogue and reactions following on cue at speed, building to the climax of Miss B's wild and shrill 'Beeeeeeep'.

(31) Miss B can become quite hysterical like Violet Elizabeth Bott of 'Just William' fame!

(32) Patronisingly and exchanging irritated glances, hit her. Fast and totally together. The daughter's reaction must be larger than life.

(33) This word is a kind of 'catch phrase' in the sketch, and should be distorted and exaggerated whenever it is used, with elongation of the sound 'aw'. On repeat of awful, all the Binges should look at each other in horror.

(34) Mr B moves behind the Pilot, who *must* keep a straight face, as it is his seriousness and resignation, combined with Mr Binge's absentmindedness, which raises the laugh. Don't be tempted to overdo it though! The following speeches should echo his tone of voice, rather self-righteous!

Miss Binge	*(Smugly)* And *I* go to Sunday school.
Mrs Binge	We always help the needy.
Mr Binge	Yes, and I vote Green. Shall I tell you *why*? I believe in pre*serv*ing God's creation. (**35**)
Miss Binge	*(Leaning on Mr Binge, confidentially)* I vote Green too . . . 'cos Daddy does! (**36**)
Mrs B	*(Glares at Mr B and stands in front of Miss B as if ashamed of her)* Shut up, dear.
Mr Binge	*(Masks Miss B, who peeps round to the left of Mr)* So, er, can we come in? (**37**)
Pilot	Anything to declare?
Binges	*(Loudly and positively)* No!
Hostess	Luggage over there. *(Gesturing upstage)*
Mr Binge	Everything? (**38**)
Hostess	*(Firmly)* Everything!
Mrs Binge	*(Horrified)* Everything?
Pilot	*(Extremely firm)* Everything!
Binges	*(Crossly)* Everything? *(Wink at audience and run USC as in* (**22**)*. In unison move US, put down luggage and smuggle things up jumpers and behind backs as they speak) (See* **23***)*
Mrs Binge	Oh darling. What about the chest freezer? (**38**)
Mr Binge	*(Cheerfully confident)* Oooh . . . I'll slip it down my trouser leg! (**39**)
Mrs Binge	What about the electric meat carver? You never know when we might have a Sunday lunch!

(35) Spoken as a politician trying to get votes at an important election. Miss Binge watches Daddy adoringly as he speaks, hanging on his every word, but also hanging onto him physically. Mrs Binge nods her approval.

(36) Definitely *very* smarmy and self-satisfied. Mrs B realises that things are being exaggerated too much, and cuts in front of daughter immediately, as she speaks.

(37) Spoken as if to a small child. Both Hostess and Pilot are not amused, and stare straight out into the middle distance.

(38) Lean forward in unison to emphasise the horror and surprise at having to leave everything. Also the next four speeches must be very fast, on cue, without losing the different tones of voice. Tone of voice and facial expression are vital in this sketch, otherwise the comedy is totally lost. It all depends very much on action and reaction.

39) A jolly reaction from her husband as he mimes the action, staggering as he pushes the imaginary chest freezer down his trouser leg. Again, facial expressions important here too.

Mr Binge *(Exaggerated horror)* Well, I'm *not* putting *that* down my trouser leg! (**40**)

Mrs Binge *(Irritated)* Very funny dear! I'll put it in my pocket then! (**40**)

Miss Binge *(Stamping foot, tearfully)* What about Teddy? I can't *possibly* go without *Teddy!* (**41**)

Mr and Mrs *(Exasperated. Look at each other, false smiles and advance on her)* Down the hatch. (**41**)

Miss Binge *(Panic stricken)* But I can't eat Teddy. (**41**)

Mrs Binge *(Impatiently grabs 'Teddy')* Oh well, shove it up there then. *(Pushes it up her jumper)* (**42**)

All Here we go. Through the pearly gates. (**42**) *(They move DS, gates open as they tentatively, and rather guiltily, try to step through)* (**43**)

Hostess/Pilot *(Loudly)* BEEEEEEP!

Binges *(Hurriedly step back in a tableau of shock)* (**44**)

Mr Binge *(Angry and surprised)* Beep?

Hostess *(Matter of fact)* Beep.

Mrs Binge *(Incredulously)* Beep?

Pilot *(Firmly)* Beep.

Miss Binge *(Shrilly)* BEEEEEEEEEP! (**45**)

Mr and Mrs *(Hit her)* Shut up! *(Miss B reacts sulkily)* But we can't give up everything we've worked for!

Hostess *(Pause. Sigh)* You must give up *everything*. (**46**)

Pilot *(Firmly)* Possessions *not* allowed! (**47**)

(40) Embarrassing adult 'showing off' and thinking he is terribly clever. Reaction from Mrs B, speaking patronisingly, like a mother to a silly child.

(41) It helps if she builds up the wailing before she stamps and speaks, as it focuses the audience's attention on her. It shouldn't be prolonged, but forceful. Danger . . . wailing can often cause the words to be swallowed, so take care! Mum and Dad's reaction must be timed and practised so that they act absolutely in unison, moving towards her on either side, so that they are very close to her. She must look terrified and tearful . . . and SQUASHED! Mr and Mrs freeze threateningly as she says her next line.

(42) This line is spoken in 'game show host' style, forced and exaggerated.

(43) This series of actions needs to be carefully rehearsed, so that the breaking of hands coincides exactly with the toes over the line, etc., otherwise the whole thing will look messy, and everyone could end up in an undignified heap on the floor!

(44) A swift tableau here with the dialogue and reactions following on cue at speed, building to the climax of Miss B's wild and shrill 'Beeeeeeep'.

(45) Miss B can become quite hysterical like Violet Elizabeth Bott of 'Just William' fame!

(46) The look they give each other must be ferociously determined. Then a fleeting smile as they draw the audience into their confidence as before with an exaggerated wink. After the wink, it is effective if they lean back, cartoon fashion, as if Tom and Jerry like they are about to give chase, *then* move immediately into the 'Push' position, and freeze with great effort on their faces. It is important that they appear to be pushing on a flat surface, so make sure all the hands are on the same plane (to coin a phrase!).

(47) Miss B moves into puzzled 'thinking' position. This line is a vital one which must be delivered clearly, and with a 'wide eyed' look addressed to the audience.

Binges *(Knowing wink)* PUSH! *(Attempt to push gate, which remains shut)* (**48**)

Pilot *(Commandingly)* STOP! *(Binges in frozen tableau of pushing, horrified looks)*

Hostess *(To audience)* It is harder for a rich man to enter the kingdom of heaven.

Pilot *(Addressing audience)* Than it is for a camel to pass through the eye of a needle!

Miss Binge *(Moving slightly out of the frozen tableau. Innocent)* But that's impossible! (**49**)

Hostess/Pilot *(Look at Binges, then at audience)* Precisely! (**50**)

Frozen tableau of shut gates, puzzled daughter and pushing parents (**51**)

(48) Refer here to Quick Pics, and make sure that different levels are used. Facial expression vital here.

(49) Once she has moved out and spoken she remains in a freeze.

(50) The timing of the two looks must be exact and not laboured. The two freeze with a quizzical, but pleasant expression, and a simple hand gesture with the free hand. When a gesture like this is made, make it definite, and hold it at the point of energy (see *Focus Freeze* in *Develop Your Skills*).

(51) Hold the freeze for three to four seconds.

Glossary

Another Culture **Style** Take a theme and transfer it from its own context into another, e.g. The Parable of the Good Samaritan – as a western! Or in modern times. Any other style can be used alongside this.

Blocking Roughly planning out the moves within the stage area, and pencilling them in the script. Be flexible, they may have to be changed.

CS *(Centre Stage)* A position right in the centre of the acting area.

CSL *(Centre Stage Left)* A position a little to the left of the centre of the acting area.

CSR *(Centre Stage Right)* A position a little to the right of the centre of the acting area.

Characterisation Taking on the outward appearance and inner feelings of another person.

Cue A word or visual signal of some kind which indicates either a reaction or another move or response from an actor or technician.

DSC *(Down Stage Centre)* A position in the middle at the front of the acting area nearest to the audience.

DSCL *(Down Stage Centre Left)* A position at the front of the acting area, left of centre.

DSCR *(Down Stage Centre Right)* A position at the front of the acting area, right of centre.

DSL *(Down Stage Left)* A position at the extreme left of the acting area, at the front nearest the audience.

DSR *(Down Stage Right)* A position at the extreme right of the acting area, at the front, nearest the audience.

ocus a. The words or actions upon which you wish the audience to concentrate.
b. The concentrated attitude of the actor bent upon his task, without being distracted.
c. The highest physical point of energy of an action.

eeze Suspended animation, total stillness, usually focused on a point of energy.

eeze Frame Suspended animation of a group of actors, rather like the 'stills' in a film sequence.

Levels

A series of positions in the acting area, which places the actors in a visually interesting position in relation one to another and also creates focus, and reveals status in their relationships as characters.

Masking

One actor standing in front of another and preventing the audience from seeing or focusing where they should.

Melodrama

Melodrama reached its peak during the Victorian era and its stock in trade was stereotypical characters used to moralise and uphold the *status quo*! The plot was usually set to a format involving the villain, usually Landed Gentry (who stalks the stage with an exaggerated step, the epitome of evil!), taking advantage of poor heroine (sweet and simpering, given to sudden fainting and exclamations of 'Woe is me', exaggerated movement, many sighs and an aura of innocence), who often had a drunken father, and reaches a crisis where she must be rescued by the upstanding hero, often in the armed forces! 'Father' (usually in an alcoholic haze, with a violent temper) often repents and reforms! The audience were highly involved and encouraged to hiss, boo and cheer at appropriate times.

Mime

Action without words.

Mime and Narration

Action without words, accompanied by a story teller.

Music and Movement

Dance or mime accompanied by music and/or movement.

Neutral

The state of 'being yourself at rest', not fidgeting, or drawing attentio to yourself, or becoming another character. It is a state of non-acting, c waiting, relaxed, but in readiness, in readiness for action when the nee arises. It is a stillness, a temporary 'being laid aside'. Stillness is reall important, and is very different from being in a 'freeze', which is ofte tense and definitely 'focused'. Stand with feet slightly apart, hands b sides.

Pantomime

A style developed from the *commedia dell'arte,* which has been adapte in Britain as a means of telling fairy stories through drama, using clowr ing and slapstick, interwoven with the fight of good over evil, and usual containing a romantic heroine, a principal boy (played by a woman) an a dame (played by a man).

Quick Pics

A small frozen group tableau representing a scene, situation or idea.

Rhythm and Rhyme

A style which uses poetry or rhyme, and makes the rhythm a feature the presentation.

Song and Dance

A style which uses songs and dances as the basis of a presentation.

Styles

Melodrama
Mime and Narration
Music/Sound and Movement
Pantomime

Rhythm and Rhyme
Song and Dance
In another Culture

Tableau A still group picture.

USC *(Up Stage Centre)* A position at the centre back of the acting area.

USCL *(Up Stage Centre Left)* A position at the back of the acting area and slightly to the left.

USCR *(Up Stage Centre Right)* A position at the back of the acting area and slightly to the right when facing the audience.

USL *(Up Stage Left)* A position at the back of the acting area to the extreme left of centre, when facing the audience.

USR *(Up Stage Right)* A position at the back of the acting area to the extreme right of centre, when facing the audience.

WIP *(Walking into pictures)* An exercise where the whole group creates a picture, as if in a frame on a given theme, concentrating on relationships between the actors within their situation. It must be an interesting visual communication. It must accurately communicate the theme, and show thoughtfulness by the actors in terms of their positioning and levels and their sensitivity to the action and mime of others.

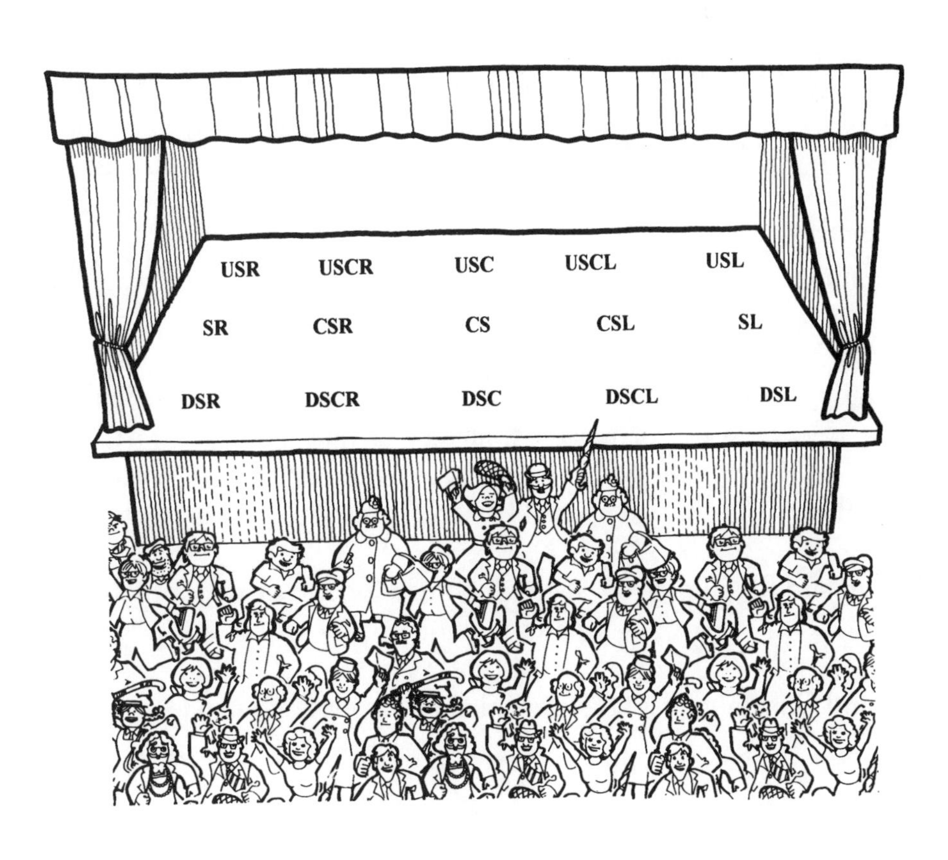

Appendix

Stage directions for use with 'Noah's Rainbow' sketch

Noah *Hands palm down, at waist level, elbows bent, sway arms from left to right. Bend knees in time.*

All **Doo**by do **doo** dooby **doo**by **doop** doooby dooby
Left *Right* *Left* *Right*

Dooby do **doo** dooby **doo**by do **doo**
Left *Right* *Left* *Arms in air, palms to audience. Feet slightly apart*

We're singing in the **rain**
Wiggle fingers and bring hands back down to waist level by 'rain', palms down.

We'll **never** be the same
On 'never' turn palms upwards, elbows bent, shrug shoulders.

What a **fright**ening feeling! It's . . .
Both hands to either side of head in 'Frustrated' action, on 'fright'

Really a pain
Dismissive gesture, towards audience, palms down, wrists bent downwards

I don't think it will stop
Wag index finger of right hand on each beat

It **goes plipp**etty **plopp**etty **plipp**etty **PLOP**
Jump Kick left Jump *Kick right Feet apart on 'plop'*

We're **drown**ing, just drowning **in the**
Palms down, fingers almost touching, elbows bent, wiggle fingers, raise hands and elbows up above head as if drowning. On 'in the' make expansive circular movement finishing in 'Dooby' position as before.

Dooby do **doo** dooby **doo**by **doop** doooby dooby
Dooby do **doo** dooby **doo**by do **doo**
As before (You can do it double speed if you can synchronise!)

Old **Noah**'s got a **boat**
Jump to left on 'Noah', faces to audience, arms stretched forwards, rowing in time to the rhythm.

It **really** gets my **goat**
Row forward Back

What a **frust**rating feeling
Hands in air on 'frust', wiggling fingers, turn to audience

That **he'll** stay afloat
Slap thigh on 'he'll' with right hand, principal boy style!

If **only we**'d been **good**
Head bent, ear to shoulder, first to left (only), then right (we'd), then left (good)

God **would**n't **have sent this flood**
Shaking heads exactly together in rhythm

We're drowning, just drowning in the **rain**
Palms down, fingers almost touching, elbows bent, wiggle fingers, raise hands and elbows up above head as if drowning. Exactly as before, but finishing with hands in air on 'rain'.

Other music included in the sketches

Dooby Do Doo – to the tune of 'Singing in the rain'
The Sun Came out – to the tune of 'Raining in My Heart' – Buddy Holly
Rainbow – to the tune of 'Rainbow' from the children's programme of that name
My name is Shadrach – to the tune 'By the Rivers of Babylon'
The Sand Dance
Rock Around the House to 'Rock Around the Clock'
Na na na na na – to a blues riff

Other books by Anne Collins published by Kevin Mayhew

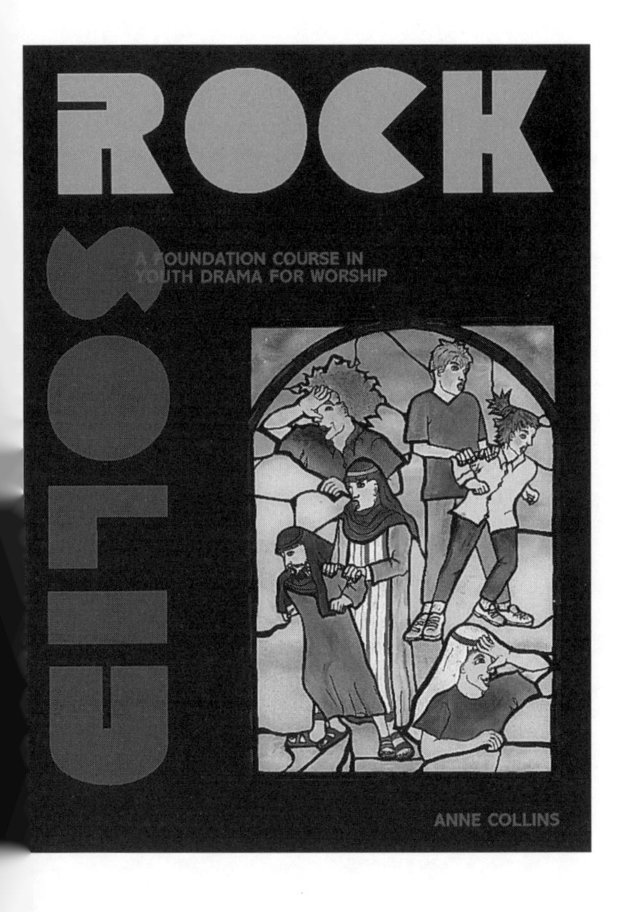

ROCK SOLID

ANNE COLLINS

A revolutionary approach to developing youth drama in worship.

This superb handbook condenses all the essential drama skills into three main areas:

- Workshops which include drama skills and ideas which focus on the theme of the following sketch.
- Scripts of original tried and tested sketches on Old and New Testament themes.
- Tips which run parallel to each page of script and enlarge upon stage directions.

1500160 1 84003100 X

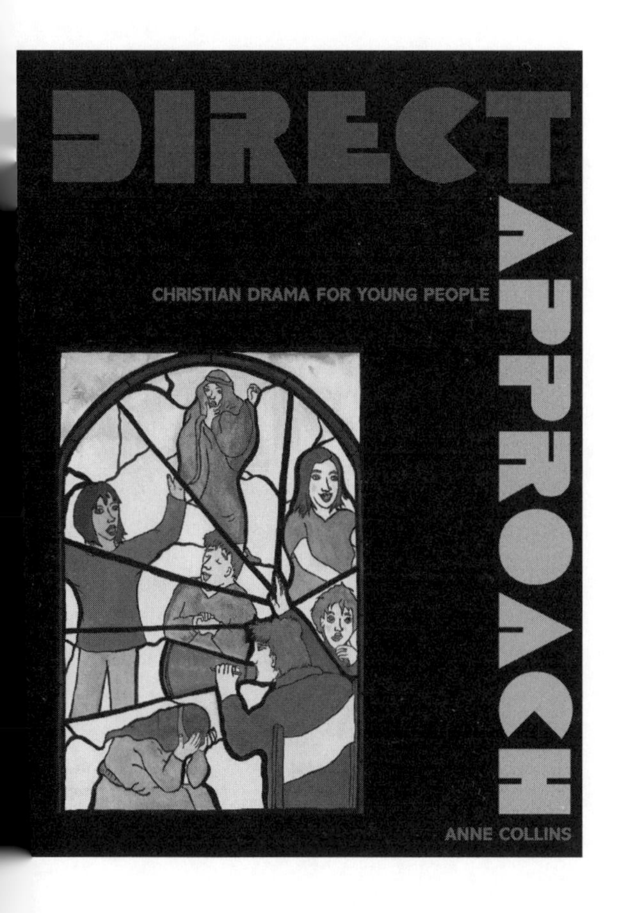

DIRECT APPROACH

ANNE COLLINS

Following on the success of *Rock Solid*, Anne Collins continues to develop her innovative approach to drama in worship for young people.

With Director's tips, workshop ideas to develop dramatic skills, and a collection of simple yet surprisingly effective sketches, this book is the perfect solution for the enthusiastic, but inadequately prepared, youth group.

1500215 1 84003 229 4